TY MATTHEWS

I hope you enjoy reading this book as much as I enjoyed writing it.

2016

TY MATTHEWS

AARON DOUGHTY

TATE PUBLISHING
AND ENTERPRISES, LLC

Ty Matthews
Copyright © 2016 by Aaron Doughty. All rights reserved.

No part of this publication may be reproduced, stored in a retrieval system or transmitted in any way by any means, electronic, mechanical, photocopy, recording or otherwise without the prior permission of the author except as provided by USA copyright law.

This novel is a work of fiction. Names, descriptions, entities, and incidents included in the story are products of the author's imagination. Any resemblance to actual persons, events, and entities is entirely coincidental.

The opinions expressed by the author are not necessarily those of Tate Publishing, LLC.

Published by Tate Publishing & Enterprises, LLC
127 E. Trade Center Terrace | Mustang, Oklahoma 73064 USA
1.888.361.9473 | www.tatepublishing.com

Tate Publishing is committed to excellence in the publishing industry. The company reflects the philosophy established by the founders, based on Psalm 68:11,
"The Lord gave the word and great was the company of those who published it."

Book design copyright © 2016 by Tate Publishing, LLC. All rights reserved.
Cover design by Samson Lim
Interior design by Gram Telen

Published in the United States of America

ISBN: 978-1-68097-693-9
Fiction / Westerns
16.08.31

1

The Dakotas
Indian Territory

It was bitter cold outside, and I could hear the storm gnawing against the side of the cabin. The wind was steadily pounding against the peeled logs and exposed eaves with icy fists. Piles of snow were drifting against the walls and windowsills with every relentless gust. The storm raced past the cabin with a force that made the southern tornados of home seem like mere windstorms. The large trees outside, rooted deep and standing strong and tall, were possibly the only reason the small cabin was not completely leveled by the wind crossing the Dakota Territory like a runaway locomotive.

The year was 1851, and I truly thought that the world was ending for me on this very night. I'm from away down south near the ocean somewhat east of New Orleans, and

I ain't never tried to live through any storm this loud and violent that could freeze bones at the core.

I lay cold and miserable in my bunk going over the events that forced me to run and eventually lead me to this cabin. I'm not normally a fighting man, but it appears to me that if you try to run from a fight, then you'll always be on the defense. I would much prefer being in the offensive, and most times that's the way I imagine things to go, but in reality, I've never had the confidence in myself to push back. And if I did, then I could pick my own time and place of battle, and sometimes, I think that might make all the difference.

This time, however, I had tried to walk away. No, that's not exactly true. I had turned my tail and ran. That's how I felt anyway. It would not have been to my advantage to push back against a drunk and violent crowd at the time; although, sometimes, certain things are worth standing your ground for. Like my innocence, for example. But it's awful hard to make a persuasive argument when you're swinging by a rope with your boots five feet off the ground. So I left. In a hurry. And once I started to run, it took away all my reasoning that told me to stop when the situation was in my favor. Like I said, always on the defense.

As I lay there in the dark shivering in the cold, I made up my mind. This is my time and place. I was in the right. I had the law on my side, and I was through walking away. I would just have to see if I still felt this way when I came face to face with the Lanauxe brothers again. But to tell you the truth, in this storm, I wasn't sure I would survive long enough for them to find me.

The storm had been battering this frozen country for three full days now and showed no signs of weakening. Most of the first day of the storm, I had been traveling the icy slopes along the Missouri River into the land of the Lakota and Sioux Indians. When the snow got too deep for my horse to make for easy travel I dismounted and started breaking the trail for him. That might be the only reason that I spotted the trail leading from the river.

There had been a fair description of the area over a campfire about three months ago back in the Louisiana Territory. According to those long-ago directions, I was to follow the trail from the river up the path through a sandy draw toward the sandstone bluffs and continue along the tributary creek for eight miles to an old prospector's cabin. The problem I was having now was that I couldn't always make out the location of the path because of the snow drifting across in front of me, so I was mostly trusting the way the land sloped and a fair amount of raw instinct to pick my directions. When I began to stumble from exhaustion and nearly being frozen solid, I remounted and trusted my struggling horse to keep me on the trail, or at least close to it. I had to urge my old horse to keep moving, but after a while he just stopped. I got down and started walking again—and he surely didn't like it—but he followed me along anyway. After an hour, I couldn't even feel my feet hitting the ground, so I struggled back into the saddle and started the roan toward the patches of shallower snow. He had been lunging and hopping and fighting the deep snow so much that I had to hang on with my hat pulled low and my head tilted into the wind just to stay aboard.

I guessed it to be around four in the morning by the time I finally rode into the small opening where the cabin stood and we were both plumb worn out. To be totally honest with you, I have to admit that it was the horse that found it. I had my chin on my chest and was swallowing a fair dose of self-pity when he came to the clearing and stopped. He even had to hump his back in the cold to get me to realize that we had stopped.

The cabin turned out to be just what was described to me. A snug, solid-looking structure with a low-pitched roof covered with earth. Of course, now it was also topped with more than two feet of snow as well.

There was a porch that was held up by two peeled spruce poles covering the front of the cabin. What surprised me most were the solid wood planks of the porch. I know these boards weren't hauled in from elsewhere, so whoever built this place, they had intended to stay. There was a sight of work done here by knowing hands. But how long had they been gone and would they come back and find me here for I had no plans of going any further for a while?

There were no tracks in the snow around the porch, but in this weather, I wasn't expecting any. With the snow drifting everywhere, there may well have been a full Indian war party lying in front of me under the snow and I wouldn't have seen it. Of course, they would have been frozen if they were crazy enough to try it now.

Aside from the tracks, I was also looking for any smoke from the chimney pipe or candlelight filtering through the windows and cracks around the loose-fitting door. There was none, although it was still before dawn and there was no reason for a body to be up and about this early in a snowstorm. Even so, I was still cautious, but truthfully I didn't care. I wasn't long from being frozen solid and was on the verge of thinking that being shot might be a welcome relief.

At least the wind wasn't as severe here in this hollow as it had been on the trail, but there was still snow blowing around with each swirling gust. If anyone was going to find me here, they would surely have a job of it. But right at this minute, I didn't care either way. I was that done in.

As I circled the cabin, I found a sort of enclosed shed back in the trees that would provide shelter for the roan. Once inside, I took a chance and struck a match to look around. The musty odor told me that this place had been long unused and there weren't any signs of fresh manure on the floor.

I found an old tin can that had been cut into a candle holder on a shelf by the door. It still held about-an-inch-long stub of candle. I struck another match and lit the candle and explored deeper into the dark structure. It was much more than a shed. This was an actual barn.

There were two stalls, side by side in the back, about four feet wide and eight feet deep each. To my right, there was a door that led to a side room that was half full of hay that looked like it had been cut years ago. To the left was a door that opened into the small corral behind the barn. When I forked some of the hay into the stall, the roan acted like it was made of fresh oats, and he went right to work on it. Of course, there hadn't been much in the way of browse along the trail under the snow and no time to search for it either.

It was a good thing for me and the roan that whoever cut the hay took the time to build a tight-fitting door on the room to keep out any roaming critters and the like. Good for him because it was ready food and good for me because it meant that I only had to worry about food for one of us.

After examining the structure, I could tell that the builder was a craftsman with pride in his work. Each log was fitted snug and tight with a kind of tongue and lap joint that I had never seen before. Not that I was a much-traveled man with any great knowledge of such things. I could surely tell though that this gent weren't no greenhorn. I made a vow to study it better in the daylight, but then again, the cabin was probably built by the same hand. I still had seen enough so far to be honestly respectful of the hands that had built here.

After I had given the roan a short, quick rubdown with a piece of an old canvas blanket, I blew out the candle and replaced it on the shelf. Grabbing my rifle and bedroll, I closed the door and latched it tight to keep out the wind, and only then did I make my way toward the cabin.

On occasion during the extreme cold when the wind blows, you can hear limbs breaking with sounds like gunshots. I could hear them breaking occasionally now from the wind and the heavy snowfall. While that makes it easier to gather wood for the fire, the punishing temperatures also keep the animals burrowed up in their dens to survive, making hunting almost impossible. Fortunately, I still had about three days' worth of supplies left in my poke, if I stretched it a might. And stretch it I would. If this weather keeps up, I would have no choice.

As I stumbled back around the cabin toward the door, I swung out wide next to the trees. For one, to make double sure that I was still alone for I'm not a trusting man, and, for two, I could get a fair idea of the immediate surroundings for defense purposes. Feeling somewhat safe, I hooked a hand around a large chunk of limb that had fallen during the storm and dragged it closer to the cabin.

I stumbled when I stepped up onto the small porch. I was more tired and worn than I could ever remember. Catching on the shelf. I placed it on the table and waited for my eyes to adjust enough to peer into the depths of the corners.

There was a bunk against the back wall with a small stove just in front of it. It was positioned so the back wall would reflect heat onto the bunk. There was a wood bin near the stove and to my relief it was almost half full.

After warming my fingers in my armpits, I was able to loosen the drawstring that held my hat on and unbuckle the leather belt that I used to keep my coat closed tight. I used a bit of the dry tinder that I always carried in my pocket and some small twigs from the wood bin to get a small fire started. After making sure that the stovepipe was clear and drafting well, I added larger chunks of wood to start warming the room. There's nothing worse than coming home to a bird nest in the pipe and you have to put out your fire and clear it.

Coming home, I thought with a wistful smile. I could only dream of a home. It had been so long since I had a place to lay my head each night that I didn't have to pay for. I had no possessions besides a worn-out saddle, a horse to tote it around, and three guns.

My guns consisted of a well-worn .54-caliber Hawken rifle and one of them new .44-caliber Walker Colt revolvers. This was the new one that Samuel Colt had designed in 1847 for Cpt. Sam Walker of the Texas Rangers, and I still had my old Harpers Ferry flintlock pistol in my saddlebag.

I could see the day getting lighter through the frozen window when I spread my bedroll on the bunk and lay down heavily with a groan. I felt that I had never been so tired. Extreme cold can do that to a body, as well as being out all night on the trail in a snowstorm.

I slept most of the day through. The only time I moved was to get up twice to add logs to the small stove.

Toward the evening, I got dressed and went to the barn. The roan was glad to see me, although I'm not sure if he was lonely or just hungry. I slipped a rope over his head and turned a half hitch over his nose to form a makeshift halter with a lead rope then I led him through the door into the snow. I leaned my rifle against the inside of the door and picked up my ax and headed to the stream we had followed to get here. I judged it to be about three hundred yards through the trees, but the way I felt then it might as well have been a mile.

I kicked a trail through the knee-deep snow, leading the roan. He was nearly as worn out as me, so he didn't mind me breaking trail for him. After about an hour of kicking and stomping my way through the drifts from one clearing to the next, we finally reached the stream. I tied the roan to a low-hanging branch and walked slowly out onto the ice. I paused with each step and tested the ice with my weight, keeping a sharp ear out for cracking and popping that would indicate thin ice.

After fifteen feet or so I realized that the ice seemed as solid as the frozen ground along the trail. With my boot, I kicked a spot clear of snow and used the ax to chop a hole in the thick ice. After I cleared the ice chunks from the hole, I led the roan forward and let him drink. It was quiet, but the wind still worried the frozen branches. The storm had passed and now it seemed to be getting even colder.

Twice the roan lifted his head and shook the water from his muzzle. I had my eyes roaming the trees across the ice-covered stream when I suddenly turned cold inside. I realized that I had just cut my defenses in half when I left the rifle at the barn, and that was not a mistake I could get away with unless I was shot full of luck.

I had six shots in the Colt pistol, but I didn't have the range that the rifle gave me. I had figured that there was no reason to saddle the roan since I was just going to the stream and back. I should have brought my saddlebags too, which held my flint and steel, extra powder and ball, some jerked meat and salt, and a few other small items that would make survival possible if I got in a bind. I had better learn to stay prepared or I wouldn't last no time in this country.

I was still looking for movement or signs of life when the roan nudged my elbow with his nose. At least he seemed to be enjoying the rest.

When he had finished drinking, I led him back to the barn. After closing the stall gate, I forked in some more hay and rubbed down the roan again to warm him and remove the snow and ice that had fallen on his back as we passed through the trees. I tried to talk to him about our situation as I rubbed, but he lowered his head and closed his eyes, so I figured he wasn't listening to me anyway.

I picked up my rifle and went back toward the stream to fill a wooden bucket I had found in the barn. I was moving quietly down the path when I suddenly stopped. I had the feeling that I was being watched. I took a slow look around, but all I could see was snow and ice. The only movement was the heavy, ice-covered branches swaying in the wind.

After a tense moment, I moved on, but I was still ever watchful.

As I got close to the edge of the stream, I noticed fresh tracks. Tracks on top of mine.

It looked to be a large wolf that had come out of the trees and onto our trail. By the look of it, he walked out just as bold as you please, right in my earlier tracks to the edge of the stream and drank out of the hole that I had cut in the ice.

There had been no more than thirty minutes past between watering the roan and my return. That meant that the wolf was still close by and I had been out here without my rifle. I slowly turned again and scanned the trees along the trail. There was a second set of tracks leading back into the trees close to the same spot where he came out.

That big lobo had to be laying up in the trees watching us. Most likely looking to make a meal out of me or my horse. If he stayed around, then we would have trouble. I suppose that hunting in this kind of weather was just as hard for them as it would be for me. Except that I probably wouldn't eat a wolf, but I'm sure he would not feel the same about me. I kept looking over my shoulder as I headed back to the cabin. Hopefully, the concentration of the man smell around the cabin and the barn would help keep the wolf at a distance.

After I set the bucket inside the door, I went back out into the fading light of the evening to gather some more wood. I had the limb that I had dragged in the day before, but it is extremely dangerous to use an ax in this kind of cold. With the wood frozen solid, the ax could deflect off of the hard surface and cut through a boot or even a shinbone. That is not a situation that I needed right now, although if I couldn't find already-cut wood, I would have no choice.

I kicked through the snow piles along the edge of the porch and found nothing. On the north side of the cabin, the snow was drifted about three feet deep, so I checked the south side and the east end first. I looked toward the barn, but that was too far from the cabin for easy access in the winter. My last hope for a wood stack was under a snowdrift.

Using a broken snowshoe that I found in the cabin, I started to dig next to the porch on the north side of the cabin. I used the wide toe end of the shoe to dig down two feet then used the heel end to probe deeper into the snow in hopes of feeling logs below. The first seven or eight feet revealed nothing. Then I felt something. With further digging I was able to uncover five logs. I could only assume that the original wood pile started at the porch and ran along the north wall toward the rear of the cabin. Since the west end was closer to the cabin door, the wood had been used from there first, leaving the remaining wood farther from the door.

By then it was almost completely dark, and after scraping and pounding most of the ice from the last of the logs, I carried them inside. I used the rest of the clean, dry wood from the wood bin to build up the fire and cook a small meal. I sat next to the stove as I ate and then cleaned the frying pan.

I was completely exhausted again, and the heat from the open stove door felt good. My eye lids were growing heavy, and I just wanted sleep. And I thought briefly of sleeping on the floor next to the stove, but I had slept on the ground so much lately that I figured I'd just wear that bunk out in the coming days. I filled the stove for the night and listened to the sizzle and pop of the frozen wood as I closed the door.

The wind had picked up again, and according to the feel of the air and the bite of the wind, the temperature seemed to be dropping steadily. It had been around ten degrees when I first went out earlier. By the time I had my meal finished, it was closer to ten below and falling. The wind was straight out of the north and steady.

I hung up my gun belt and my hat and sat on the edge of the bed. I set my boots close to the stove and dove under the blankets. It didn't take long to fall asleep once I was able to stop shivering and lay still.

I woke once just after midnight and listened to the mournful wail of a wolf in the distance, howling balefully into the moonlight. I was wondering if he was still alone or if he was calling in reinforcements as I drifted back into sleep.

In the morning, I awoke shivering to find that the cabin had been invaded by the cold. It had been a long, cold, bone-chilling night, and while it never was in me to lay in bed after daylight, I was not ready to face the morning because it would be another long, cold, physically painful day. I tentatively reached an arm out into the cold room, and I nearly put my hand on the metal of the small stove before I detected any heat from within. I was not wanting to leave the slight warmth I was able to maintain under my blankets, but I knew I was going to have to get up and coax the fire back to life before I completely lost all the coals, and I surely was dreading it. In this kind of cold, at forty below, sometimes even the fire will just give up trying to survive and simply die from sheer exhaustion.

I looked worriedly at the few logs that I had placed by the stove. As a testament to the unrelenting cold temperature,

I could see a couple of logs that still had ice on them even though they had been inside the cabin next to the stove all night.

As much as I wasn't looking forward to the task ahead of rustling wood, I always recall what my pa told me the day we had to shoot our old draft horse.

We had been using the big horse to haul logs to sell at the mill to pay our debts at the general store when he slipped on the muddy trail and broke his front leg and had to be shot. I was only ten at the time, but Pa set me down on the front porch where he liked to smoke and contemplate. I knew better than to speak when he had something worrying his mind, so I sat quiet for about ten minutes. He finally looked at me through the smoke curling up from his pipe bowl and said, "Sometimes things look bigger than they are, Ty. We still got to get them logs to town, but we ain't got a horse now. Always remember this, son. If a man don't at least try, he won't ever do." And with that, we got up and went to work.

If I recalled correctly, Pa done some trading and swapping until he had the price our neighbor wanted for renting his team of mules. It probably cost us a bit extra in time and labor, but we got them logs to town.

So no matter how hard or large the task ahead looked, I had to at least try.

I made up my mind and swung my feet over the edge of the bed. When they hit the floor and I stood up, it was like

I had just put my feet right into the frozen Missouri River. I hurried to the stove and threw in a handful of the grass that I kept for quick fires. I placed several small slivers of pitch-loaded pine on top of the grass then carefully topped that with two larger chunks of pine. I then put another log about the size of my wrist on the side so that it would roll into place as the smaller ones burned.

Leaving the stove door open so I could encourage the fire by talking to it and it could get all the air it needed, I scurried back under my blankets before my feet froze to the floor.

A flame flared bright and cheerful in the tuft of grass for a few seconds then almost burned out. It wasn't until the pitch thawed out somewhat in those slivers that it started to catch. I pleaded with the fire for a couple of minutes when it finally stood up and started making some progress. I guess being alone as much as I have been, you can find companions almost anywhere you look, and me and that fire was no exception.

I had the good sense to place my boots on top of the stove while I was up, and when I could see tendrils of smoke forming around the soles and boot heels, I figured they was warm enough to melt the ice from my socks.

After stuffing my cold feet into the almost-warm boots, I slid on my coat and turned my attention to the fading wood supply and breakfast.

I sat down at the table and dug out some jerky and hardtack from among my possibles. It wasn't the grandest morning meal, but I had started many days with worse fare than this. In fact, I can remember some days that I had to just swallow real hard to fool my stomach into thinking that I had eaten something. Most times it didn't work.

I would have to plan carefully and make every move count. I was beginning to realize just how unprepared I was for coming this far north at this time of year. But thinking back, I always get my feet ahead of my brain when it comes to planning.

After I ate, I put the last two logs into the stove then sat down in front of the open door. Trying to absorb some of the escaping heat into my clothes before I went out, I sat with my head hanging low thinking back over the last month and how I ended up here.

2

Heading north into the wild, frozen wilderness of the Dakota Territory in a hurry during winter, unprepared, and with several men hell-bent on killing me following somewhere behind, I tried to calculate my chances of survival. I had no grand illusions about my situation, but in truth I had lived most of my life from one tight spot to another. As I said, I ain't much of a planner. I had lived most of my days trying harder to get out of work than if I had just dug my heels in and got the job done. Most times I got by on luck more than skill.

Where I was now, though, plain luck wasn't going to get it all done. I would have to decide what I was going to do and stick to it, where I would go when the weather warmed, if it ever did. I also had to remember that those two Lanauxe brothers, even in their misguided ways, would never stop looking for me. How do you reason with someone who won't consider all the facts or just plain don't care?

They didn't know—or maybe didn't want to know—about the true circumstances of the fight that killed their pa. They had their version of the story, and I couldn't prove it right or wrong. They wouldn't listen anyway. They had it in their head that I shot the old man in the back after we had some heated words, and I had to admit that's what the evidence looked like, but it was wrong. I had to get clean away from them or face them, and if they kept looking, then the getting-away part was out.

They both came from a cutthroat gang of thieves ran by their father, the late Virgil Lanauxe. Everyone knew him as Doc, and he made his own rules in the swamps and bayous of the Louisiana Territory. His gang had a hand in everything that they could make a dime off from Baton Rouge along the great Mississippi River all the way up to Natchez and didn't give a hoot whether it was legal or not. He ruled with an iron fist and a lynch rope and was rumored to have paid for a few shootings as well.

They were known to run a few trading ships along the east coast and around the tip of Florida to the ports of New Orleans and were suspected of flying a few pirate flags when the cargo they were after was worth enough.

I just wanted shut of them. I wasn't wanted by the law even for questioning and, well, let me just tell you what happened back in New Orleans and let you decide for yourself.

Doc and me had some words over a buckskin horse I had just purchased. I told him I had bought it from the hostler at the livery barn. He claimed it wasn't theirs to sell. I had just handed him the bill of sale that I got for the horse when I caught a movement behind him. I yelled as I lifted my rifle, for I had seen the glint of light from a gun barrel. There was a shot from the shadows that hit Doc in the back at the same time I stepped sideways and shot at the stab of flame. The shots sounded almost as one. Doc turned toward the shadows where the shot came from, took two steps in that direction, and fell on his face. Dead.

One of the Lanauxe thugs came around the corner just as he was falling away from me and then looked at me in shock as I stood there with a smoking gun barrel.

There was quite a crowd already gathered when the marshal finally showed. I explained the situation and told them why Doc still had my bill of sale in his hand when they turned him over. The marshal let me finish recounting my version and looked over in the shadows but found no sign of anyone else. Doc's man that seen him fall wasn't telling his version just like it happened. He claimed that I shot Doc while he was walking away, and that's when he stumbled and fell dead. He also claims that there was no second shot.

Since the bullet didn't go all the way through Doc's body, there was no blood on me or on the ground until after he fell.

Even as bad as Doc had treated most of the folks there, the marshal couldn't find anyone who would agree with my statement. Most folks were glad to be rid of him but still not willing to speak against the rest of the gang.

The deputy collected my guns, and I was removed from the crowd and escorted back to the jail for further questions. The marshal arrived about twenty minutes later and sat down heavily at his desk. He took off his hat and ran his hand over his balding head while wrestling with his thoughts. He picked up the coffee cup that the deputy had just set down and winced as his lips met the steaming liquid.

When he spoke, it was in a slow, quiet tone. "You said your name was Ty Matthews. Am I right?" I nodded, and he continued. "Well, Ty. I'm Tidwell, Marshal Lane Tidwell. You probably done most of those folks out there a favor that they will never understand. Doc has been getting mighty brave and a lot meaner lately."

I held up my hand and said, "I done no one a favor. I didn't shoot him." He started to speak, but I cut him off and said, "You seen the sign, and I told you just like it happened." I stood up because I was getting mad. I leaned forward on the desk and asked, pointing in the direction of the alley, "Did you find the footprints in the alley like I said?"

He shook his head. "Sit down, Ty. There's got to be a thousand prints in that alley. It's the shortest way from Spencer's store to the saloon. Everybody that come to town goes to the store and the saloon."

"I'm not going to be saddled as the guy that shot anyone in the back. Even someone as bad as Doc," I said in obvious frustration. "There's got to be some evidence that sides with me. It's the truth."

He raised both hands in mock surrender. "Okay. Okay. I've got some more looking around to do, but you're going to have to wait here." He stood and started around the desk. "I'm not going to put you in a cell unless you make me, but you can't leave this office till I get back. The law has a process that I must follow."

I stood and turned toward him as he crossed to the door. "I'm willing to give the law its due process just so long as it finds the truth."

He turned his head to look at me over a pointed finger and said, "You just stay here until I get back."

When the door closed behind him, I went to the stove and filled a cup with coffee. I dragged a chair to the space between the stove and the wall that separated the cells from the front office. I sat down and leaned back against the wall carefully so as not to spill my cup and prepared for a long wait.

The deputy stood up and stretched. "There's a couple of empty beds in them cells if'n you wanna stretch out." He jerked his thumb toward the back of the jail.

"No thanks," I said. "If I ever get locked down without being guilty, it ain't going to be an easy thing. I'll make do out here."

He grinned and replied, "Suit your own self then. I'm bushed."

I heard the floorboards creak on the other side of the wall as he entered one of the empty cells. The leather straps creaked noisily as his weight descended onto the cot. It was less than a minute that I heard the first snores. A few minutes more and it sounded like a grizzly bear choking on an angry badger. About ten minutes in, the straps protested again as he turned on his side. That old griz' must have finally swallowed that badger because he sounded much calmer now.

After a few minutes over two hours and several cups of coffee later, I heard boots on the boardwalk outside the front door. There was a short pause then the door opened, and the marshal came into the room in a hurry.

"Ty, we got troubles," he said as he crossed to his desk. He opened the desk drawer and retrieved my pistol. It was and old Harper's Ferry flintlock pistol, so I lifted the frizzen and checked the charge in the flash pan before I tucked it behind my belt.

He went to the gun rack and pulled down my rifle as he spoke. "I spotted enough tracks to believe your side of the story. And I found a new bullet furrow in the back wall of the store just about where you said. Only it was farther down than I thought. Since the bullet that killed Doc didn't go all the way through the body, your bullet must be the one that hit the wall." He handed me my rifle and belt knife. "I also spoke with Zeb down at the livery. He said young Ben Lanauxe traded him that horse for the last two month's feed bill. That confirms that your bill of sale is good. I guess Ben never told Doc about the trade."

I never had a chance to reload my rifle so I ran a swab down the barrel and began loading it as he continued, "Some of Lanauxe's men are talking up a lynch party." He looked at me kind of embarrassed. "I'm the law around here, and I'll do everything that I can. But there's no way I can stop twenty armed men at once." He crossed the room and looked out into the street. "I'll file the report with the territorial marshal and state my findings so you won't have any trouble with the law, but you're going to have to leave town now or stay locked in a cell so I can protect you. I'm sorry, Ty, but that's all I can do for you."

"Well, I ain't about to let you lock me up when I ain't committed a crime, so I'll just take my chances out on the trail."

While he looked up and down the street from the window again, I asked, "Am I going to have a problem with the law if I have to defend myself getting out of here?"

"Not from me," he said. "As long as what you do is in self-defense, but I don't hold with needless killing." He went to look out of the window. "That's the reason I took this job in the first place—to protect the town and stop the killing. And I will eventually find out who killed Doc. I may shake his hand right before I lock him up, but he will still stand trial."

He turned his back toward me and continued, "I've a boy bringing your horses around back, but it's going to take a while since the livery is right across from the saloon where the crowd is gathered."

I looked up sharply. "I hope he ain't trying to ride that roan. He won't make it fifty feet before he's on his head in the dirt."

The marshal grinned. "No. I had old Zeb saddle your horses, and I told Timmy to lead them behind his own horse. That will usually help calm any rough horse, and I wasn't sure about yours."

He thought for a short moment as he sipped his now-cold coffee. He made a face and set the cup down hard in disgust. He looked up and said, "When you are ready to go, you can go out the back. I'll go out the front and sort of distract the crowd a mite. That should give you plenty of time to get away."

"Marshal," I said, "I don't like the notion of running when I've done something, so I'm even more against it when I ain't." He turned from the stove and started to speak, but I held up a hand and continued. "I know what you're saying. I'll leave on your say-so. But I'm saying, on the record, I ain't running. I'm leaving because you and me agree that it's the best thing to do right now."

He smiled with relief and said, "It will be reflected in my report that I issued you a mandate to leave town before more trouble started."

Just then, there was a light tap on the back door. It was a young, gangly, blond-haired boy of about ten that I took to be Timmy. The marshal gave him a few coins and patted his shoulder. "Ty, your horses are ready." He gestured with a finger and said, "Go into the trees just past that old barn to the spring then turn left. Follow the runoff from the spring to the first draw you come to on the right. When you get to the head of the draw, you will find a trail leading toward the west. About five miles down that trail, you will be in Ash Valley. It's not the usual route, so that crowd won't think of it right off."

Timmy smiled proudly as he handed me a sack and said, "Mister, my ma put in a chunk of roasted side meat and some bread in that there sack." He followed me as I moved to the door.

I turned and said to the grinning boy, "Thanks, Timmy. And thank your ma too but, how did your ma know I needed this?"

The marshal said, "I asked her to throw together a bite of grub when I went to see if Timmy could get the horses for you."

I thanked Timmy again then looked at the Marshal and asked, "Where can a body lay in some supplies seeing as how I can't do it here?"

He waved toward the door and herded me outside. "When you get to the south end of Ash Valley, take the trail across the creek and head due west. There's a traders' post at the bend of the river."

I lifted the stirrup and fender of my saddle to check the cinch while he explained, "It's ran by Josh Nolan and his wife, Carol. Tell them that I authorized an emergency ration of supplies for you. If they ask what the emergency is, just tell them to ask me later and that you can't talk about it. Josh and I have an arrangement."

"An arrangement?" I asked. "Does this happen enough that you need an arrangement?"

He looked up sharply with a jerk of his head. "No. Not this anyway. There is more than one reason to need to be prepared. Look, Ty, I know you don't like this any more than I, I can't change—"

Suddenly, there was a shout from the street in front of the jail. "Marshal! I know you can hear me in there."

The words were slurred with whiskey but loud and clear: "Let that back shooter come out here and try me." Then another voice said, "I'll even turn my back and give him a fair chance too." Several bellows of drunken laughter followed.

The marshal stepped in close and grabbed my arm. He spoke in a low, urgent whisper. "Wait until I get them talking then go. This may be your only chance." As he turned, he told Timmy to get on his horse and get out of sight but to do it quietly.

I waited to a count of ten then heard a loud, calm voice say "Frank, don't you boys have something more important to do than keep folks up with all this noise in the street?"

I took that as my signal and mounted the roan. I pulled the reigns to the left until we were facing down the alley to the south. I could still hear shouting from the street, but I was hoping that the marshal had the situation under control. I had about thirty feet to go before I could turn right around the corral and barn toward the trees. I hoped no one was watching.

I started the roan at a slow walk with the lead rope for my spare horse and the reins in my left hand, keeping my right hand gripping the rifle across my lap in case of need.

As I passed the space between the jail and the barbershop, I could see into the street in front of the jail. I could only see the edge of the crowd but enough to know that there was at least twenty people raising a ruckus.

Then I happened to look across to the boardwalk on the opposite side of the street. I saw two men standing on the boardwalk. One was leaning against the awning post, and the other was standing, arms crossed, watching the crowd. The latter was in a pin-striped suit and had one of them fancy derby hats on his head. The leaning man was in range clothes, but they looked fairly new.

They weren't part of the crowd so mayhap they were the reason behind the crowd. They may have bought a few rounds at the bar and quietly made a few suggestions about justice or lynching to get the talk started. Sometimes in a quiet town, that was all that was needed.

Fortunately, the alley that I was in was mostly dark, and there was an oil lantern hung on the post at the front of the jail. Its glow would prevent anyone from seeing me from the street because it is almost impossible to see into the darkness after staring at a light.

I turned away and started walking my horses past the next building when a man came bursting out of the space between. He had a rifle in his hands, but it was in the crook of his arm and not in a position where he could get it into action. It seemed that he was even more startled than me because when he skidded to a stop after seeing me, he just stood there and let me hit him in the head with my rifle barrel. When he fell to the ground unconscious, I simply turned my horse to the right past the corral and disappeared into the trees toward the spring.

There was close to a quarter moon hanging in the sky with middlin' cloud cover, so at times it was hard to pick out the best trail down in the canyon. I had to give most of the responsibility to the roan as we picked our way along.

I was in unfamiliar territory at night, with a hanging crowd looking to put a rope on my neck. I had no intention of stopping, but it almost seemed just as dangerous to continue on in the dark. Well, maybe not, but it seemed so at times. If the roan stepped off into a wash, we'd both be done for.

The runoff from the spring worked its way back and forth along the bottom of the canyon. The path was also strewn with boulders and brush, making me backtrack more often than I was comfortable with. I kept an ear out for the sounds of pursuit and paused often to listen. I also watched the ears of the horses knowing that they would sense things well before I would.

After an hour of fast travel, I came to a clearing in the brush. Maybe it would be better described as a small opening in the debris I was traveling through. There was sparse patches of grass that the horses found immediately, and I dismounted and switched my saddle to the buckskin gelding. The roan didn't like it, but I didn't stop long enough to ask his opinion anyhow. I think he was just jealous.

I did tell him later that as long as he didn't go and die on me, I had no reason to find a new horse. I think it made him feel somewhat better.

3

That's how this all got started. At least it's the beginning of how I ended up here in the cabin.

I got up and walked out of the cabin on to the small porch and into the cold wind. I paused for a quick scan of the ground close to the cabin for new tracks in the snow then another scan farther out. Nothing but smooth new snow any direction that I looked. I went down the steps and across the frozen white expanse toward the barn. Finding no tracks there either, I went inside to check on the roan.

When I opened the door I could hear a soft nickering from the roan, but because it was so dark in the tightly built barn, I was momentarily blind.

I stepped inside and swung the door wide to let in some light then waited for my eyes to adjust.

When I could make out the roan's outline, I spoke quietly to him as I walked forward to the stall rail. I scratched under his mane and patted his neck, and in return, he nipped at my elbow to let me know that he didn't appreciate being locked up in the dark.

I wanted to discuss our situation, but he's never been much on conversatin'. I opened the stall and put the bridle over his head and buckled it in place. I brushed the hair down on his back before swinging the blanket in place.

I do that out of pure habit now, since one time back at home, I didn't take that precaution, and after a long ride, there were sores on the back of pa's old plow mare's. Pa really gave me what for, and I never forgot it.

I swung the saddle in place and threaded the latigo through the cinch ring then back up to the front rigging ring. I made several loops with the strap and pulled it tight, but I waited a bit before I tied it off. That roan wasn't fooling me when he blew out his chest while I was cinching up. I waited about a three count then jabbed a thumb in his belly back toward his flank. That gets him every time. He jumps and blows, and I grabbed the latigo strap and cinch her on down. I couldn't afford to have a loose saddle, but I can't blame the roan; he was just looking for a more comfortable ride.

I led him outside and closed the door behind us. I walked him fifty yards down the trail, studying the ground for tracks and generally looking around before I mounted up. I decided to take a roundabout path, so I turned the roan into the trees and made a large, sweeping circle that would put me near the watering hole. I was heading to the stream to water my horse, but I didn't want to make it a habit of going right to a place without scouting around. I was thinking that there was probably many a dead man who now thought the same.

As soon as I left the trail, I spotted the track of that old lobo. His trail told the story of his seemingly pointless wandering in the trees. But I did notice that each place his trail doubled back was at location where the cabin was clearly in view.

That sneaking sidewinder was watching me. I instinctively glanced quickly left then right, but snow and trees were all that I could see.

Since I hadn't even laid an eye on him, I couldn't say he was hunting me—curious, maybe. I'd have to be watchful. Not only for him but for them gents that was hunting me also.

I worked around so that we entered the trail just a few yards from the place I had watered the roan the day before. Dismounted and untied my ax from behind the saddle. While my hands were busy untying the leather straps, my eyes scanned the far bank. When I looked downstream, I thought I caught a bit of movement in the brush.

I didn't stop moving my hands, and I kept my head straight. I moved my eyes away then back to the spot but could see no more.

When I walked up to the frozen place where I had busted the hole before, I made sure I was facing the brush where the movement had been. It took only three good swings with the ax to reopen the access to the water. I knelt down and took off my left glove. I scooped out the ice chunks with my left hand then quickly wiped it on my leg to get the water off before it could freeze. I held my hand under my arm inside the heavy coat to rewarm my fingers before putting the glove back on, my eyes always moving back and forth.

I led the roan to the water and let him get his fill, and I found myself stamping my feet and rubbing my hands to keep warm. If I was any judge of weather—and I'm not— I'd say it was still below zero. At least the wind had died, and the snow had stopped falling.

I mounted and headed upstream through the trees, and I let the roan set his own pace as I scouted around. We stayed deep in the trees because at least there, the drifts were no more than two feet at most. In the open area along the frozen stream, there were drifts that stacked higher than seven feet in some places.

I came up to a shallow draw that ran from somewhere behind the cabin down to the stream. Normally, I don't like to get myself down into lower ground like that, with one way to run if trouble comes. And someone on the edge of the draw would have the advantage of me and could cover that whole draw with a rifle.

But with what I found down there, it was worth the chance—mostly because I hadn't seen anyone or any tracks.

There was a tall bank that had been undercut over the years by the runoff down the draw. There were several trees that had been growing straight and tall on the top of the bank. When the bank caved in, the trees fell into the draw and left a neat row of six or eight trees all piled up in the wash ready for an ax or saw. Each tree looked to be eight to ten inches through at the base. They had fallen last year, so they were dead and would be free of moisture. Since they weren't frozen solid, they would be softer and would cause less danger when the ax hits.

I found a way down that wasn't too steep for my horse and dismounted close to the dead trees. After tying the roan somewhere he could nibble on some grass that had cured on the stem, I unlimbered my ax again.

As I approached the fallen timbers, I scanned the edge of the draw with searching eyes. My eyes traveled up the head of the draw or as far as I could see through the trees and brush. There was no movement or tracks in the snow, at least none that were visible from where I stood.

I selected a tree that had fallen last; therefore, it was on top of the others, and with great care I began to cut off the root section. After cutting two lengths of about ten feet long, I rolled them to the side. Selecting the next tree, I repeated the process.

I was warming up slightly, although I was forcing myself to go slow and take care with each swing. I couldn't afford to start sweating, and one slip or mistake here with the axe could spell the death of me and no one would ever find me. At least not in time to help.

When I had six poles cut, I turned three of them so that their narrow ends were lying together. I retrieved my rope from the saddle and slipped a loop around all three. I put the next three together in the same fashion, with the ends elevated on a slab of rock so that I wouldn't even have to dismount when I came back. I could just throw a loop over the ends and take a dally around the horn and drag.

I started dragging the first load down the draw until I found a trail up that wasn't very steep. Even then, we had a struggle to get to the top of the draw. The roan was slipping on the snow and ice with every step. At one point, the logs hung up on a small tree, and I had to back up and pull them to the side before we could continue. When we topped out on the crest, we both needed a breather.

Now, a body might wonder if it would be easier to just find a log or two closer to the cabin. Well, not only were these logs mostly free of ice and snow but I was also thinking of my future struggles. You see, right now, I have a horse to drag with, and I'm in fair condition physically. That may not be the case in the future and I could just walk out and gather the close wood then.

After a slow five minutes to catch our wind, we started off through the trees toward the cabin. It couldn't have been more than five hundred yards to the cabin, but with all the backtracking and weaving through the congested trees, it felt more like a mile. We had been out less than three hours, and I was already tired again.

I guided the horse up close to the cabin and stopped. I backed him up a few feet and tried to shake the loop loose. I bounced it a couple of times, but because of all the ice and snow packing around it from the long drag, it wouldn't budge. I climbed down from the saddle, and with the heel of my boot, I was able to loosen the rope. I remounted and coiled the rope.

Just as I was about to tie the rope to the saddle, I heard a soft whimper in the brush behind the barn. The sound reminded me of a dog I used to have back home. I sat still for a minute looking in that direction but heard nothing else. I tied off the rope and eased the horse forward to the rear of the barn and peered deep into the brush and shadowed trees.

The only tracks I could see were mine from the first day and two sets from that lone wolf.

He had been right up behind the barn. By the look of the disturbed snow, he had padded to the corner of the barn where he could see the cabin and sat down on his haunches. From there, he would have had a clear line of sight to the rear and north wall where I had dropped the logs.

I would have to keep a close watch because it looked like the man smell was not going to scare this one away. If a wolf got to my horse, I would have very little chance of surviving in these conditions and even less chance if he got to me.

I know surviving is possible, and I know it has been done before. Mostly by early explorers, Indians, mountain men, and a few tough old birds who didn't have the word *quit* in them. I just wasn't sure that I would make all the right choices. I didn't have all that much experience in how to live like that, and I hadn't had the time to prepare.

The roan, growing impatient with me, blew and shook himself all over. Maybe trying to warm up in the cold air, I wasn't sure. I gave him a nudge, and we headed back to get the second load. I looked behind me once and caught sight of something darting between trees. It was too small to be a horse and too fast moving to be a man on foot, so I decided just to keep moving and keep watching.

I followed my earlier trail back toward the draw, searching for a better path to take with the next load of logs, occasionally checking my back trail. I rode right up to the edge of the draw and pulled up hard on the reins when a flurry of movement caught my eye. I had my rifle about halfway out of the boot when I realized what it was. Then it was too late.

Three deer took off like a shot up the draw to the right. They had been browsing through the brush and sniffing the wood chips left from earlier. I needed the meat but hadn't expected to see anything moving in this kind of cold, although I am the one that ain't used to it. Those deer were born here.

I booted the roan forward as I mentally kicked myself for not being ready to act. What if there had been men down there looking at signs of my presence? Then I just poke my fool head up like some ignorant old turkey. Gobble twice and wait to be shot. Yep, that's me. What a green-livered tenderfoot. I was thinking so much about what I was doing that I left all caution to the wind.

I rode up to the logs and untied my rope. I was knocked so off kilter at myself that I missed those logs twice with my first two throws. I dang near felt like a wet behind the ears kid.

I finally tossed the loop true and snugged it down with a jerk. I dallied up and turned toward home.

There it was again, "Home." What kind of a softhead was I getting to be anyway? I was getting plumb disgusted with myself. To have a home meant to own something, and what right did an old wandering saddle bum like me have to be thinking that way?

I decided to put the mental spurs to that line of thought and get back to work.

We made a little better time on the second run through the trees with a slightly better route to follow. I made sure to keep watch all around and even stopped several times to listen. I didn't like the fact that I was making all kinds of tracks that anyone could find, but I had no choice.

I pulled the logs up to the cabin and laid them next to the first load. This time, I was able to shake off the rope without getting down. I smiled. A small victory, but I would take it.

I put the roan in the barn so he would be out of the slight wind but decided to leave the saddle on. I would scout a bit more when I took him for a drink later and maybe get another chance at those deer. I loosened the cinch a bit so he could relax then untied the ax, pulled my rifle out of the boot, and headed back to the cabin.

I leaned my rifle against the cabin wall and cleared the snow from the porch to make room for my wood stack. I picked up the ax and loosened the belt around my coat.

I cut the first log into short enough chunks that would fit into the stove then split each chunk into four smaller pieces. The task was more difficult than it should have been because there wasn't a stump there to use as a chopping block. I had to stand the wood in the snow and each time I hit with the ax, the wood moved. It doesn't sound like much, but it's much easier to chop at waist high instead of at ground level. And the snow would cushion the force of the blow under the wood, causing me to have to swing more times and harder.

When the first pole was done, I carried an armful into the cabin and dumped it by the stove.

As I entered the cabin, I wasn't greeted with the wave of warmth that I had expected. I had forgotten to close the stove door when I went out that morning. The fire had been allowed to burn with no restricted airflow and had probably burned bright and hot for an hour or two. When I leaned down to look in the stove, I found nothing but ashes. My head dropped.

Disgusted, I slapped my hat on my leg. How many mistakes could I allow myself to make before one of them killed me? If I had been injured, if I had fallen through the ice, or just been overexposed to the cold, I would have crawled back here expecting a fire and probably would have died right in front of the stove.

I stood and took off my heavy gloves. It was then that it dawned on me that the wood that had been outside the cabin had lain there for at least two years, maybe more. It was dry rotted and decayed. And with the door open on the stove, it was no wonder the fire had burned itself out. That didn't make it any less of an empty-headed, rawhide, tinhorn mistake.

The wood I had just brought in would burn longer because it had been dead only a short time and was much more solid and dense. That fact didn't help me now, though.

With one of the smallest sticks of wood, I stirred the ashes around and pushed the few remaining charred chunks to one side. I raked out the cold ashes into a large tin can that had been used before for the same purpose. I used my knife to split off several small slivers of wood from one of the chunks I had just brought in. I got out the last of the dry tinder that I had in my pocket and placed it in the stove. I started laying the small slivers of wood I had cut from the log then placed a handful of small twigs on top of that. I struck a match and touched it to the tinder and watched it hungrily climb toward the wood. I gently coaxed the flame to life. I slowly added a few more of the small splinters I had just cut until I had a fair-sized blaze going. I slowly filled the stove with wood.

Satisfied that the fire would burn on its own and work on rewarming the cabin, I slipped on my gloves, gathered up the ax and my old Hawken, and then went out the door.

Leaning the rifle against the corner of the cabin where it was close and handy, I went to work cutting up two more poles. I stacked the wood on the porch between the cabin wall and the outer roof post. It would take up most of the room on the small porch, but it would also keep any new ice or snow fall from covering it completely.

I still had three poles left that I would cut up and split tomorrow, so I had at least temporarily fixed the wood problem. As long as I didn't let the fire go out again. I needed to find some more dry tinder to keep in my pocket for just such an emergency.

The evening was getting on toward dark, so after I checked the fire in the stove, I headed back to the barn to retrieve my horse. I had taken three or four steps across the yard when I stopped short. I turned around and walked back to the porch and picked up the rifle. I grumbled and shook my head in frustration at myself as I crossed the snow-covered space to the barn. "You are gonna make one too many mistakes if you keep playing the tenderfoot," I told myself.

The roan jerked up his head and nickered at me when I entered. He pushed on the stall boards with his chest and stretched his nose toward me as he smacked his lips. He was telling me that he was ready to be out in the open moving around, which is what horses do. He stamped his legs showing me how energetic and agile he was then shook his head, rattling the bridle and bit. He was ready to go.

I led him out and closed up the barn behind him. I walked over to the corral and looped the reins over the top rail. I slid the rifle into the boot then checked all the buckles and straps on the bridle then went to work tightening the saddle, all the while scanning the tree line and the trail for movement.

When I was satisfied, I grabbed the reins and mounted up. I let the roan prance a bit and hump his back in protest before I brought his attention to the fact that I wasn't going to get off and that it was he who wanted out of the barn. Once we were moving on the trail, he forgot about me and concentrated on the trail ahead.

Normally, I would lead a horse for a short distance before mounting because I felt that I gave them a chance to get loose and warmed up. It also established a routine for them so they would know what to expect each time. I'm not sure if it helped; that's just what I had been taught as a youngster.

But today, I needed to get moving. It was coming on dark, and the wind was picking up a bit. I wasn't sure if there were still wolves around and didn't want to get caught trying to defend myself in the dark against any kind of critter. Not to mention them folks that was hunting me.

As we entered the shadows of the frozen forest, I immediately had the feeling that we were being watched. I pulled my horse to a stop and listened for a moment but heard nothing around me but the wind in the treetops. There was the occasional flurry of snow drifting down as it was dislodged from the limbs above by the wind.

We started moving again, and several times I turned in the saddle to check my back trail and scan the trees on either side. Nothing. I just couldn't shake the feeling.

We continued on, and it didn't take us long to reach the edge of the slope that overlooked the ice-covered stream. I paused there long enough to see that there were more tracks from that wolf. It had appeared sometime after I had watered the roan that morning and, by the looks of it, had been back several times. I continued to the spot where the now-frozen hole was. I dismounted and looked around carefully as I untied the axe from behind the saddle.

After breaking the ice and while the roan was drawing his fill, I fastened the axe in place. When he had finished, I led him back up the bank and remounted. By the look of the sky, I had about thirty minutes before the light faded enough to make it difficult to see back in the trees. I guided the roan up the slope and into the trees about fifty yards south of the trail that we had been using. Keeping from the trail I had used before, I was hoping to spot another deer searching for something to nibble on, so I drew the rifle and laid it across my legs. Since the wind hadn't drifted the snow too deep this far back in the trees, our progress was mostly smooth and quiet.

I had gone nearly two hundred yards and spotted no tracks other than the wolf, and of course, there would be no deer in this vicinity with that much wolf sign. I told the roan what I was thinking and that I had decided to head back to the warmth of the barn. He flicked an ear back toward me to show that he had heard me, but he didn't reply.

We were about to emerge onto the trail leading back to the barn, so I pulled up under the overhanging branches of a large box elder tree. I sat quiet for about two minutes when I heard something moving in the snow across the trail. I turned the old Hawken toward the sound and patted the roan to keep him quiet and continued to watch for another minute in the fading light.

Straight across the trail from where I sat, I noticed a darker shadow in the low brush. I allowed the roan to shuffle forward a few feet and kept my eyes on the dark, shadowed area. Sure enough, it moved.

It was getting almost too dark to distinguish any shape or outline, and I couldn't just sit here wondering. I had almost made up my mind to ride out with my rifle barrel covering the brush when I heard a low, high-pitched whine. Kind of lonely and forlorn.

The dark shape shuffled toward the trail in a low crawl. It was the wolf! Or maybe *a* wolf. I couldn't be sure if it was the same one that had been leaving tracks.

He crawled on his belly in the snow to the edge of the trail then lay still with his paws laid out in front just like our old collie back at the farm. His head was held low with his ears up and alert.

He whined again.

It almost looked to me like he was wishful for some company. Well, come to think of it, so was I. Just not the kind of company that was wishful to find me.

We sat like that for a few minutes then I decided to ease forward to see what he would do. It was almost completely dark, and when the horse moved it was like he just disappeared. He turned and went into the brush with almost no sound.

The roan was impatient to be getting back and I couldn't see anymore, so I let him start down the trail on his own. I hunched my shoulders against the growing cold and turned my collar up.

We had gone about five steps when, on a sudden thought, I stopped the horse. I took off my left glove and shoved it deep down into my coat pocket. Fumbling my fingers into the small pouch that I carried there, I fished out two pieces of dried, jerked meat.

I turned and tossed them onto the trail behind the horse as sort of a social invite—to show him that I would be neighborly if he had no dinner intentions for me or my horse. Then I replaced the glove and went to the barn. I was sure that meat would be gone in the morning.

I dismounted and led the roan into his stall. I lit the candle and set it on a stall post then removed the saddle and blanket and forked in an armful of hay. As I curried the roan's back with that piece of canvas, he almost closed his eyes. His head dropped a few inches, and he sighed heavily.

I smiled and said, "I know just how you feel, old-timer."

I kept brushing until I had dried all the sweat from his back where the saddle had been. Normally, an animal can stand snow or ice on them like when it falls in a storm because it builds up on top of their coat. An animal that has been sweating from work or from a saddle could form a layer of ice next to the skin underneath the hair. Most times, their body heat will take care of that soon enough, but I figured, in this cold and if I had to saddle in a hurry, I didn't want to take the chance of having a layer of ice under the saddle.

I pitched another armload of hay into the bin then picked up my rifle and saddlebags. I carefully blew out the candle, placing it back on the shelf, and closed the door of the barn. Using my gloved hand, I pulled my collar tight around neck and ears then followed my earlier tracks across the snow and up onto the porch. My eyes scanned the edge of the trees and the open expanse around the front of the cabin, to make sure I was alone, and then I went inside.

This time, I was greeted with warmth. It most likely wasn't above fifty degrees, but when you have spent hours in the below-zero wind, even fifty was warm to the skin.

I took off my gloves and placed them in my coat pocket then removed my coat and hat. These I hung on the peg by the door. I lit the large candle that sat in the center of the table and began to throw together a meal.

I poked around in the stove to settle the burning logs then added two more to produce the extra heat I needed for cooking. In a skillet on top of the stove, I fried the last of my bacon then used the grease and some flour to make a thick gravy. I added a few hardtack biscuits to the lot and finished with a mostly full stomach. It was most shameful that I hadn't any coffee to top off such a fine feast, but I had been shut of that luxury for some time now.

4

The thought of coffee got me to thinking about the trading post I stopped at after I left New Orleans just ahead of that lynching crowd and how I had traveled into the darkness with only the hills on either side to guide me in the night.

We—me and my two horses—had made it through Ash Valley to the southern end and decided to hole up in a large stand of trees until morning, which was only a few hours away. I figured it might raise some doubt about my intentions if I showed up in the middle of the night demanding supplies. I made a dry camp and staked the two horses on a small stand of grass hidden on the opposite side of the trees away from the trail. I dozed from time to time, but I kept one ear listening for that crowd of misguided do-gooders. When there's a noose swinging in your direction, you had best not relax and let it find you.

When the light began to filter over the horizon in the east, I mounted and followed the trail west like the marshal had suggested. It was about an hour after full sunup when we crossed the creek, sure as you please, there was a trading store. It wasn't really like a store. It was more like a small barn with a house attached to the back of it. On the right past the house part, there was a newly constructed corral with a lean-to shed on one side for shelter for the animals and another for storage. On the left, there was a wide, open space of low brush and weeds with an occasional dead tree here and yon.

As I got closer to the front of the store, I could see that there was an old, weather-beaten sign above the stoop that read simply, "Dry goods and mercantile," and the word *food* had been added below it. A much smaller, newer sign on the wall that explained, "Josh and Carol Nolan, Proprietors," suggesting that most likely they had only recently come to own the place. *Or*, I thought, *maybe they just made a new sign.*

When I looked closer, I could tell that the entire building was older but had several new touches here and there. Not patches or repairs but more like long-needed, fresh changes.

I dismounted and tied the roan to the hitch rail. I tied the spare horse next to him then stepped around the rail toward the store.

I hitched my gun belt and lifted my pistol to check the load. I lifted the frizzen and inspected the powder in the flash pan. Since it had been a long, damp night, I wanted to make sure that moisture hadn't penetrated the pan, which would cause a misfire. My rifle is usually the first gun I would use in a fracas, but in the close quarters of a store, a rifle would be useless.

Even though there were no other horses in sight, except in the corral, I still used caution. I peered in the window first, and then when I opened the door, I stood mostly to one side. There was no bell above the door to jangle and announce my presence as I had expected when I went in. Maybe that was on their to-do list.

I stepped to the left behind a shelf of odds and ends as I scanned the dark interior of the store with my eyes.

There was no movement in the front of the store, but I could hear someone rustling around through a door behind the wooden counter. I moved farther to my left and went around the end of the shelf toward the counter. I was almost close enough to ring the little desk bell to get someone's attention when a woman came through the door with a broom.

She gave a startled yelp when she realized that I was standing at the counter. There was an instant of hesitation as she tried to decide if I was going to be a threat or just another customer. When I just stood there quietly and smiled, she seemed to realize that I meant no harm.

"G-Good morning," she finally managed. She stepped to her left to lean the broom against the counter and said, "I'm sorry. I didn't hear you come in."

"Sorry, ma'am," I said sincerely. "Am I a bit early for store hours?"

"Well, no. That's fine. My husband and I are early risers."

"I'd admire to buy a cup of coffee if there's one to be had," I said. "And maybe a bite of something for breakfast, if you've got it to spare."

"Yes. Of course," she said as she smoothed out the front of her apron. "We just don't get many visitors this early. Most travelers arrive in the afternoon or evening. It takes about six hours to get here from New Orleans by wagon and longer if you came from anywhere else."

"Please follow me," she said as she turned around and went through the door behind her.

"I thank you kindly, ma'am, as long as I'm not being a burden." I followed her around the counter.

"Oh, no," she continued. "It's our pleasure. I was just about to call Josh in to the table, and I know he'll be glad of the company."

She turned and gestured to a small, square wooden table with four matching, sturdy-looking chairs. "Please sit and make yourself comfortable." She pulled a thick white mug from a peg in the wall and added it to the two mugs already on the serving platter next to the table. She lifted the platter and sat it on the end of the table. She wiped her hands down her apron again and said, "I'll get the coffee. It's just behind in the kitchen."

"Thank you again, ma'am." I pulled out the nearest chair.

I started to sit down when she exclaimed, "Oh dear, forgive me"—she placed a hand over her mouth—"I'm sorry, my name is Carol." She wrung her hands together in embarrassment. "Carol Nolan. And my husband's name is Josh."

I smiled and touched my hat brim. "Mine's Tyrel, ma'am. Tyrel Mathews, but folks just call me Ty."

"Well, welcome, Ty. You sit and I'll call Josh and I'll be right back with that coffee."

I sat. I could smell the wonderful aroma of fresh-baked bread coming from the door of the kitchen. It was mixed with the smell of ham. And coffee. The rich, fragrant smell of strong fresh-ground coffee.

I heard a door creak on rusted hinges and Josh being summoned from somewhere. He must have been behind one of the lean-to sheds when I looked around during my earlier approach. I heard a muted response and an explanation on company at the table for breakfast. Then the hinges creaked again.

Carol returned with a large coffeepot and filled two cups.

"Josh will be here in a minute," she said. "I hope you don't mind waiting a few minutes. The bread isn't quite done yet."

"Ma'am, as long as there is coffee, I can wait 'til noon, if need be," I replied as I lifted the steaming mug to my lips and took a sip.

She smiled and headed back into the kitchen.

The hinges creaked yet again, and after a minute, a big man came in through the kitchen with a platter loaded with ham, beefsteak, whole, roasted potatoes, and eggs. In the other hand, he carried a large bowl of gravy. He set them down on the table as I stood and extended my hand. "Ty Matthews." I said as he set down the platter.

This had to be one of the biggest men I have ever seen. He was at least four or five inches above my six feet and would tip the scales at near three hundred pounds. His black beard hung down six inches from his chin and was generously streaked with gray, although I took him for a fairly young man, maybe in his late twenties. He had a deep, raspy voice that seemed to resonate in the room.

He wiped his right hand on the side of his leg quickly then reached forward and grabbed mine in a vicelike grip. With a large smile he said, "Josh Nolan at your service. I s'pose you've met my lovely bride, Carol."

"Pleased," I replied.

"If it's alright by you, friend, we'll make talk while we eat." He smiled. "A growing, young buck like me has got to get in his nourishment when it's handy."

We sat down and ate what I can only describe as a first-class meal big enough for a crew of four. We talked over our plates as Josh made most of the meat disappear. We talked of the weather, the trails east and west, cattle and range conditions, and such. Then, Josh started asking about ladies' fashion, hat styles and handbags, and such, and I knew he was steering the conversation for his wife's sake. Carol listened intently and kept glancing at her husband with smiles of appreciation, although it was little that I could tell them on that subject.

Halfway through the meal, she rose and went into the kitchen, and after a few minutes the bread was brought out. It was cut into two-inch-thick slices and was stacked high. It completely covered a fair-sized plate.

Josh paused long enough to cover two thick slabs with a generous helping of butter and a swirl of honey. Then he devoured the first one in four bites.

I made a fair-sized dent on my side of the table too, I'll admit.

After we finished, we sat back, and over several cups of some mighty good coffee, I told them about the marshal and how I came to ride this way.

Josh said, "The marshal saved me from a run-in with the youngest Lanauxe about a year ago, and I own him a favor." And they both said that they would be glad to help anyone pull one over on the whole Lanauxe family.

"I don't want to use up the marshal's favor. There might be a time that he would need it himself, but I sure do need some supplies."

Josh looked up and smiled saying, "The marshal and me have an understanding, so you just get what you need and come back anytime."

After Carol wrote out the list of items I gave her, I said that I would like to pay with cash, and they both glanced at each other with a sort of relief in their eyes.

Josh looked up from under his thick eyebrows and smiled. "I'd let you have the supplies on the marshal's word if need be, but we are real short on cash money right now." He drained his cup with a grin. "If you have enough cash money, I'd sell you a pretty little maid too." He looked at his wife expectantly.

Carol jumped up and slapped him playfully on the arm.

"You surely would too, you old goat," she blustered playfully.

Of course, you could just about hit the big man with an ax handle and he would take it as playful.

They bagged up my supplies, and Carol looked at me almost shameful when she gave me my total of eight dollars and twelve cents. I just smiled and started counting out the money. I looked toward Josh and said, "I'll make it an even twenty dollars if you will toss in that fresh apple pie that I smell and that Walker Colt revolver I see there."

He never even hesitated. He just leaned over the counter to the back shelf and wrapped his big hand around the gun and handed it to me. Then, he reached back down behind the counter and brought up a canvas sack and placed it in front of me. He said, "That goes with it. Might near a hundred .44-caliber ca'tridges in there."

"Thanks." I tried to trade in my old Harper's Ferry pistol on the deal, and he refused.

He made a convincing argument when he pointed out that the old, single-shot pistol was the same caliber as my Hawken and could be used if I ran out of .44 slugs for the colt.

When I started loading my supplies, Josh picked up my pack with one hand, even though it weighed over one hundred pounds, and placed it gently on the packhorse. Right then I was some glad that he wasn't one of them after me. That man would be dangerous when riled.

I thanked them both again and warned them to watch out for those that would surely follow.

I said my so longs and then struck north then swung a mite west so I wouldn't run into the Mississippi River. I was heading in the vicinity of Fort Smith and knowing all the while that no outlaw with half a brain would go near an army fort, even though it was held by the Confederate soldiers at the time.

My plan was to ride as fast as I could to Fort Smith, conduct some business that someone would remember, and plant some misleading information to throw them off the trail. Then disappear quietly in the other direction.

That night, I turned north from the trail for about a half mile then made camp in a low hollow with a small spring of cold water bubbling up between two boulders. I put my coffeepot on the coals at the edge of the fire and listened as it perked and hissed. I chose to eat only the cold meat and bread that Carol had packed because I knew that after that huge meal she had fixed, I'd only be disappointed with my own cooking. But I could make coffee with the best of them. And I washed it all down with apple pie.

I had made a fairly secure camp and sat in the dark wondering when they would start looking for me and how I would react. I had grown up on a farm in the hills of Virginia and, in all my twenty-six-or-so years, had never been a wanted man. Not from the law and certainly not from a vigilante crowd. I was scared.

Not from the fight and not even from those who sought me, even though they would likely kill me on sight if they caught me. No, sir, I was scared more from the injustice and not being able to protect myself when I had done nothing wrong. Being railroaded, so to speak. It could almost make a man lose his faith in the law—and even society in general—if they weren't willing to give a man the benefit of innocence until he had a trial and evidence presented. And it has always been my experience that vigilante crowds aren't interested in the law or justice. No, sir. No matter how you sliced it, they were only interested in revenge.

My situation was starting to feel hopeless, and I went to sleep that night with more questions than answers in my head. I was really getting scared.

I was startled awake around midnight by the sound of running horses in the clear, still night. I knew the sound was from the trail I had been on to the south, but that's all I could tell. I mentally kicked myself for not thinking about hiding my tracks where I left the trail. They may not find my trail in the dark, but they would be back in the morning, and they surely would then. I pushed the coffeepot back into the coals and began to break camp.

I took my time packing, even though I had little to organize, and when I was done, I sat down and finished off the coffee and the pie then rinsed and loaded the pot. I can't be sure that the movement on the trail was men actually looking for me, but I had to assume that it was, and in my mind, that took away all doubt about my situation.

I sat under a tree and dozed until daybreak, and then I climbed into the saddle and took the lead rope a turn around the horn and headed northeast. It was close to noon when I topped out on a bald ridge to look in the direction of the fort. I was looking for the best and easiest trail to descend from the low ridge I was on when I heard the loud slap of a bullet hitting the tree next to me. It was a full two seconds for the sound of the report to reach me, which meant that the shooter was on the next ridge to my south.

Even though there was a pause before the report came, I knew the source of such a sound and was moving instantly. I spurred the roan and went over the crest into the canyon beyond at a full gallop with the packhorse in tow. I never got a chance to see if there was more than one man on that ridge where the shot came from, so I would have to assume there were several.

They would expect me to go north or west, which was my intended direction, so I went east up the canyon then south until I crossed the very trail I had used yesterday then turned west. I followed the trail but stayed well south of it hidden in the trees and pressed both horses for speed.

It took me seven days of hard riding and very little rest or sleep to reach Fort Smith. I stopped long enough each day to take care of the horses and alternate my saddle and pack between them. My pack weighed around 100 pounds, and I am at 180, so the pack was probably a welcome relief. I did stop on the 4th day before dark and rested them both for 5 hours. I guess I was feeling a little guilty because I didn't even know if I was being followed or if they were ahead of me. On the other hand, if I was being followed, I would have a chance to lose them before they had an opportunity to get close to me.

5

When I rode into the southern edge of town, I was immediately met on the road by a deputy. He was a tall, thin man with dark, curly hair with a gray streaks at the temples. His clothes were neat and clean but were far from new. His mustache was so thick that it covered his lower lip, and the corners drooped to each side and ended in long sweeping curls. At first glance he looked uncomfortable and somewhat comical on the rawboned horse between his knees, but that old Greener shotgun took the laugh right out of the situation. It was a short, double-barreled model with two exposed hammers under his right thumb. The dark walnut stock lay across his right thigh, and the twin bores looked right at me as he spoke. "Morning, stranger."

I pulled up and sat quiet and still. This was his show, and I was content to let him call the tune.

He shifted a little, and I noticed that the shotgun never wavered from my chest. "Where you coming from?" he asked.

I let my horse shift to the right, but the shotgun followed as if by magic.

I responded in a low tone, "Is it your custom to pull a gun on someone before you know if he's friend or foe?"

He chuckled. "I'm still alive, ain't I?" He waited ten seconds to show he meant business; the twin barrels drifted six inches to my right. "Better?"

"It's a start," I said and started my horse forward.

He hove on the reins, and his mount backed up and turned the horse's tail to his right to block me again. "I asked who you are, mister."

When his horse backed around, it put his Greener pointing off the wrong side of the saddle to cover me.

"No," I said as I drew my pistol, "you asked me where I was coming from."

He stared at me with cold, hard eyes, calculating his chances. He decided they were absolutely zero. I could see the realization in his face.

I holstered my gun and said, "Now that we're even, let's talk." He still eyed me with suspicion, but he waited, making no attempt to move his shotgun toward me. "Marshal Lane Tidwell of New Orleans sent me over this way." While it was not the full truth, at least it wasn't a lie either.

His relief showed plainly on his face. I don't mean he was scared; I don't believe that for a minute. He had been outfoxed by his own move, and I had saved him the trouble of figuring a way out without dying.

"Sorry, stranger," he said. "I'm guessing if you was one of them, I'd be facedown on the trail right now." He turned his horse to face up the trail toward town. "There's been talk of some gents coming to stop the hanging tomorrow." He gestured with a nod of his head up the trail. "It's time for my night relief to show. Come up to the jail, and I'll buy you a cup or two."

"I'm always up for one. The second one depends on how good you make it." I smiled.

I'm sure he was thinking that he had me outfoxed right then. He was getting me up to the jail where he had help. If I was a no-account, he would have me then.

Right then, I didn't care. I was tired, my horses was plumb tuckered out, and I was hungry.

He didn't speak again until we pulled up to a low-roofed building with the word *Jail* painted over the door. As he dismounted, he said, "My name's Mason. That there loose-footed galoot on the porch is Randall. He's my relief tonight."

I eyed the young lad reclined in the chair next to the door of the jail. He couldn't have been more than eighteen, and I could tell at first look that he carried a large chip on his shoulder.

I stepped down and paused as you well know is common for a body that spends long hours in the saddle. So as not to let it show, I fussed over the saddle a bit. Then, I tied the two horses to the rail.

I walked inside, and as I filled a cup from the pot on the stove, I started formulating a new twist to my plan. Well, maybe not new, but another bit of false information. I grinned while I sipped the hot brew.

The one that called himself Mason filled a cup and limped across the room.

"Mason," I said as he found an empty chair behind the desk, "I just thought I may know those hombres you talked of. I had a run-in with two characters down south of here." I sipped and paused like I was in deep thought.

Mason lowered his cup to the table and said, "If'n you got it to say, then out with it, man."

I grinned inwardly. "I stopped last night at a fire about ten miles down south of here. I was just looking for some grub that I didn't have to cook myself and a cup of coffee. There was two gents at the fire, but by the look of the camp, they had been there a couple of days. At first it was nothing, but after I was at their camp for a couple of hours, I heard one say that they had to be shut of me before they got to town. The other said he thought I might be carrying some money and that they should take it."

I walked to the corner of the desk and put the bait under his nose. "I'm sure they were coming here, and they are two bad men." Then I proceeded to describe in great detail the men on my trail—the Lanauxe brothers.

Mason looked hard at me and asked, "Did they try to rob you?"

"No," I said, "the big one said that their other job was more important than a few dollars from a no-account drifter."

Oh, they swallowed the hook all the way. Then I added that they may send others in first to scout around so they would still be ready in case any real outlaws showed up.

They followed me to the restaurant across the street, and I laid on the story that I was in an awful hurry to get to San Antone and that I was going to be moving fast as can be and that I had urgent business to attend to. Over our meal, we talked about the trail conditions to the south, and I could tell Mason was trying figure out where I had come from by my description of the conditions to the east. When I realized this, I started relaying things that I had heard from others about trails north and west as well.

When the meal was done, I decided to get them fully on my side and bought their meals too. I said, "If you boys ever get down south of San Antone, look me up. I can always use a couple of good, solid men on my spread, and you both look as capable as any I've seen." I smiled genuinely. "Look me up at the Rafter M."

With that, I thanked them again and left.

I told the hostler the same yarn about business to the south when I sold my spare horse to him, and I even asked him about part of the trail condition. He would surely remember that.

I had wanted a spare to carry my pack, but since this horse was tied directly to the people that were after me, I decided I would pick up another one later. Not to mention the fact that I made an additional twenty dollars on top of my original purchase price.

I repacked my supplies into a smaller bundle, added a few items from the general store, and then tied it behind my saddle. I headed out of town just like the hostler said to go. The trail turned south after about three miles, and I kept going straight west into the trees for another two miles then turned north and started hunting a place to camp. I would sleep like a dead man tonight because I was confident that the Lanauxes wouldn't reach Fort Smith tonight, and when they did they would have quite a reception waiting for them.

I found a bluff where a great slab of rock had fallen in the distant past. It had wedged itself against the bottom of the bluff about ten feet high. The lower end of the slab was about ten feet out from the bluff, creating a ten-by-fifteen covered shelter.

I just wanted to lie down and sleep, but I knew I had things to do first.

I gathered a handful of twigs and broken limbs and got a small fire started inside the shelter. I positioned my fire so that it was mostly concealed by a cluster of cedar trees growing close by. I picketed the roan at the other end and would rely on him to warn me if anything moved that I should know about.

It was close to midnight when I laid my head down and pulled the blanket over me. I must have been really trusting of that half-broke bronc of a mustang for I slept hard. Chances are, he probably slept too when he was supposed to be watching.

At daylight I felt better than I had in a month. I was also hungry as a starving mule, but I had been there before. I didn't want to get slowed down by cooking several times a day, and I could push myself harder than anyone from New Orleans. I would survive on hardtack, jerked meat, and a bag of hard candy that I had picked up in Fort Smith.

6

That was the beginning of how the trail over many long, hard miles led me to this cabin in the snow. And thinking back on how I got here makes me wonder how much each small decision we make affects the outcome of our future.

I used the last piece of hardtack to wipe up the remaining gravy from the skillet then cleaned up the remains of the meal and put everything away.

I stuffed more wood into the stove and lay back on the bunk. It was still cold in the cabin, but the heat still was enough to feel good after the long hours outside. I felt my body slowly relaxing and the tensions of the day draining away. I knew that I would have visitors soon; it has always just been a matter of time. I tried to make a mental list of the things that needed to be done in the coming days.

I needed meat. I had just eaten the last of my side of bacon, and I only had two chunks of dried meat left. I also needed flour, sugar, salt, cornmeal, and the like, but what I needed most was meat. And coffee.

I would also need to continue to build on the wood stores that I had started. Maybe after I move on, another traveler might show up in a bad way and be needful of things. I would do my part for him. I had reached many line cabins that had a fire laid in the stove or fireplace so that all I had to do was strike the match. Some even had dried meat and dried vegetables ready to go in the pot and just add water and set it to boil. These things could save the life of a needful man.

I instantly froze.

I heard crunching footsteps in the snow. Then I heard some movement on the porch. I stood quietly and drew my pistol. Easing toward the door, I paused to listen and heard nothing but silence.

The noise I heard earlier didn't sound large enough to be human, but nothing else would come right to the porch. Unless it was a bear. There would not be anything short of a cannon that would prevent a bear from coming through the door if he happened to be of the mind to come in.

I listened at the door for another five minutes and was rewarded with more silence.

I put on my coat, in case I had to be outside too long, and I stepped to the side of the door and lifted the latch string up. As the door swung open, I crouched and pivoted around the doorjamb and peered into the darkness with my pistol in my fist. The porch was empty. The rectangle of snow illuminated by the dim moonlight was empty, except for my own shadow and the footprints I had left earlier.

I stood and took one step through the door and looking left then right. There was no movement in sight. I was about to search around the side of the cabin when I looked down and noticed wolf tracks right there on the porch.

I was beginning to think that this wolf had been someone's pet at one time. I had never heard of a wolf getting this close without attacking. But this wolf had shown no signs of attack. If anything, this wolf was acting lonely.

That was crazy. Yet here were the tracks on the porch, and there was the whining and crawling to the edge of the trail earlier today. I went back inside, took off my coat, and sat down on the bunk. I had my hands on my boot to pull it off when I changed my mind. I stood and went to the peg where my coat hung and pulled out one of the last two chunks of dried meat. I opened the door and tossed it on the porch.

Turned back inside, pulled off my boots and laid down. I was almost asleep when I heard the same scratching noise on the porch. Then silence. I rolled to my side with a smile and slept.

The next morning, I awakened just before dawn by the rumble of thunder in the distance. Today, I would hunt. I needed to scout the area as well, and with a storm coming, at least the new snow would cover most of my tracks, but it would cover the tracks of any animals too.

An experienced tracker could still find a trail even under the snow. All he had to do was look for the small ridges where the snow was kicked aside. He could also dig down to the original snow where it had been packed by the weight of a boot or a hoof. The best trackers, however, could guess at the decisions you would make and go where you would go and only occasionally need to see your footprints in the snow.

I oiled and cleaned my Hawken and then my Colt. I put a handful of extra slugs in my pouch and a filled my powder horn. I put the last piece of dried meat in my pocket and filled my canteen.

The water would freeze, but if I got myself in a bind I would at least have some water when I put the canteen next to a fire.

I stepped out into a cold, still, quiet morning. I could see where the wolf had returned to the porch to pick up the dried meat. There were no other new tracks in the snow around the cabin, but I figured he was around somewhere. I crossed the now-packed snow to the barn and opened the door. I was greeted by the excited nickers from the roan as he shook his head and pawed the stall door. I leaned the rifle against the wall beside the door and swung the stall gate open and put the bridle over his head before he could push past me. I secured the buckles and wrapped the reins around the top rail of the stall and began brushing his back. After a bit of impatient prancing and sidestepping, he finally held still because he really enjoyed the rubdowns. Maybe it was just the attention that he liked.

After I got him relaxed and all smoothed down, I swung the blanket and saddle in place and cinched it down. I slid the rifle into the boot on the saddle and led the roan outside into the cold of a new day.

I paused for a moment and went through my mental list of things that needed doing so I could have it all straight in my thinking before my brain started to freeze. After a bit, I mounted with the decision to get a few things done so I'd have less to consider on the list for tomorrow.

The roan was eager to be moving in the brisk morning air. Our first stop would be at the water hole, but I was trying not to be predictable in my movements, so I decided to move upstream and cut a new hole in the ice.

I had my rifle out for a quick shot if I spotted any game, but I couldn't leave my glove off for very long. I would have to make the best of any opportunity that came along, so I kept my hand loose in the glove so I could throw it off in a hurry.

The rumble of thunder was much closer, and where there is thunder, there would be lightning strikes. The only parts of the storm that concerned me was the lightning and the wind. Each one could be a dangerous proposition in the right conditions, but together, they could be downright deadly.

It was too cold for rain, and that in itself was a good thing. In this cold, it would only be heavy snow, but if the wind came along, then it would get bad in a hurry.

I followed a shallow runoff depression down to the edge of the ice-covered stream about a mile north of the original trail where we had watered the day before. I sat my horse in the shadows for a while before venturing out in the open. There was no movement, and the only sounds were from the approaching storm.

I was beginning to like the solitude and the quiet, but the cold is more difficult than a body might think. But living during the summer months had its own set of problems too. Either season can be dealt with, if you have the knowledge and the skills to survive. And it helps to be prepared, but that is not always possible.

I unlimbered from the saddle and walked out onto the ice with my rifle resting across my left arm. There was a thin spot in the snow where the wind had funneled down the draw and blew it away. Some places were drifted four to six feet, but here, it was about six inches. I used the edge of my boot and cleared the ice in a two-foot circle.

Walked back under the trees where I had left my horse and slipped the rifle into the boot and untied the ax. Now I wasn't much on long-range defense with an ax, but this was a necessary risk. There was no cover here if I were attacked even if I had the rifle in my hands the whole time.

It took almost ten minutes to cut a hole in the ice because it was over ten inches thick here and I had to be careful, but the water finally came rushing in.

I removed as many of the ice chips as I could from the hole before my hand became numb. Then I went to get the roan. I tied the ax in place, and because I was still trying to warm up my hands, I left the rifle on the saddle.

After the toan had all the water that he wanted, I led him back into the trees again. I had been keeping a sharp lookout for any movement that might suggest meat, but even though the storm had let up somewhat, the temperatures were still brutal. Even wild game likes to stay holed up in bad weather.

My hope was that they had to get around and forage for food just like me and that our paths might eventually cross. It would then be up to me to take advantage of the situation when it appeared.

I noticed some small tracks in the snow near the edge of the ice and several narrow trails leading across the stream. It looked like there were several small animals moving around close to what used to be the water's edge.

When I was around ten or eleven years old, we had lived near a Cherokee family who ran trap lines for food and furs to sell or trade. They had a boy that was eight at the time, and he taught me how to make bait sets, snares, deadfalls, pitfalls, and spring traps. I decided to use some of that knowledge now.

I led my horse up the slight bank and into the trees and tied him to a low limb. Reaching into my saddlebag, I took out a bundle of rawhide strings and peeled off several pieces, four to six feet long. It had been four or five years since I had needed to use traps or snares, but once you learn a thing, it's easy to recall it when necessary.

I walked along the edge of the stream about ten feet back in the brush until I found a well-worn path with several sets of tracks that sort of funneled down tight in one spot. I crouched to the side of the funnel and fashioned a loop in one of the rawhide strips, almost like a small version of a Mexican riata. I grinned. Only this one wasn't braided. With a small, thin twig, I suspended the open loop over the trail with an opening about four to five inches across. Then I tied the other end to a low bush. I had just made a drag snare. The animal steps through the small opening in the center of the loop, disturbing the string, and causing it to fall onto their back, and as they try to walk away, it simply tightens around them. The more they pull and fight, the tighter it gets. As long as it's anchored to a sturdy object, it will hold a fair-sized critter. This works good for the slower-moving game and doesn't usually need to be baited if it's placed on a trail.

The next one I set was called a *spring snare*. It was nearly three hundred feet further down the bank.

I came across a well-used trail through the brush. Almost all of the tracks were those of a pine marten. Or maybe a family of martens.

Now it's easy to assume that a marten prefers pine nuts because of their name, and that's true when nuts are available. But the truth is that they like to eat small mice, rats, and moles too, and that's when I remembered the dried meat that I carried. The martens would love that.

I'm not sure what they were after here, but this trail full of tracks means that they have found something close by. And I've found that when you're setting a snare or trap, you can't be too choosy about your opportunities. You have to take what's offered.

I started by locating a thin, young sapling, about two inches at the base, that was close enough to the new trail I had found. I bent the tree over to see where the top would meet the ground, and that's where I put my snare. I let the tree go for now and got started on building my trap.

I selected two small sticks and cut them down to about ten inches long. I packed down the snow at the edge of the trail, and with the butt end of my knife, I drove the two sticks into the ground about four inches apart with three inches sticking up above the snow. I cut a notch in each stick so that the notches were facing each other. Then I cut another small stick—called the trigger stick—so that it fit loosely into the two notches I had just made. When I put it all together, it made a short *H* in the snow. I was ready to set the trap.

On the trigger stick, I tied the only piece of the dried meat that I had left. Then I bent the tree over and straddled it so that my hands were free. I tied one of the rawhide strings to the top of the tree and made a loop in the other end. About a foot up from the loop, I tied my trigger stick in place then held it in the notches as I slowly let the tree back up. When the rawhide came taunt, it pulled the trigger tight in the notches and held the tree in a curved arch providing the spring pressure needed for the trap. Then I cut a heavy limb from a nearby bush and placed it behind the bait so it could only be approached from the front. I adjusted the loop so it was directly in front of the bait, and any animal trying to eat the dried meat would be standing in the loop.

Hopefully, when it pulled on the bait, it would release the trigger, and I would have fresh meat for supper.

I retrieved the roan and circled wide through the trees and headed past my two snares and deeper into the forest. I decided to head back to the draw where I had cut the wood the day before to see if those deer were back. Since the previous storm had dissipated, there seemed to be more and more animal movement, so I was optimistic of my chances for success, and I set several more snares along the way. I was really hopeful that this new storm would not be as severe.

The last trap I set was really just taking advantage of a natural opportunity where a large log had fallen between two trees. Here, I would make a deadfall trap.

I lifted the log and used a stout limb between the two upright trees to hold it up out of the way until I had a trigger built. I used the same setup as before with the spring snare by driving two sticks into the ground with the two notches and inserting a crosspiece for a trigger. The main difference here was that I didn't have anything for bait, so I set the two sticks about eight inches apart and used a longer trigger stick. I used a low limb on one of the live trees as a support and draped the remaining rawhide string over it. I secured the rawhide to the log, and making sure that it wasn't twisted as it passed over the limb, I tied it to the trigger as well. I should explain here that I tied the rawhide about an inch from one end of the trigger stick, and this was for two important reasons: The first was that I didn't want the string to be in the way as an animal tried to cross the trigger. The second was that it would put most of the pressure in one end of the trigger, making the other end much easier to knock loose from its notch.

Using my knife, I dug around in the earth between the trees and then shaved some bark from the trunk, exposing the green flesh underneath. Any animal passing by would hopefully smell the fresh turned soil or the exposed bark and investigate for a free meal. When they stepover the trigger, it should dislodge and release the log above.

I seated the trigger stick in place and held it there with my boot toe. I then placed my shoulder under the log and lifted it to remove the limb I had used for support. I eased the weight of the log down until the rawhide was stretched tight, and then I moved my foot from the trigger and backed up. I used a few small limbs to block the openings on either side and behind the trigger so any investigating animal would have to cross over the trigger.

I surveyed the job and made a few minor adjustments with the limbs surrounding the trap. When I was satisfied, I remounted and moved through the trees toward the mountain. Actually, it was just a very tall hill compared to the ones from back home, but they were at least five to eight hundred feet up to the crest.

I kept my eyes to the ground studying the new tracks that I found in the snow. I saw tracks of rabbits, birds, squirrels, and even the lumbering trail of an opossum. Now, I had never eaten an opossum, but I do remember a time or two that I would have been glad to try. Teeth, tail, toes, and all and would be soaking the juices with the hide. Well, maybe. Anyways, I was real hungry once or twice.

The roan moved slowly and, as far as I could tell, fairly quietly through the trees. But how quiet can you really move when you are sitting on top of a thousand-pound animal?

Quiet enough I hoped.

We worked our way within sight of the draw where I had cut the trees, and I could see the trail that we had left while pulling the logs over the edge and back toward the cabin. There were tracks on the ground from mice and birds and what looked like a ground squirrel, but nothing big enough to eat and, more importantly, nothing human.

I eased the roan forward until just my head cleared the snow-covered edge and I could see down to the bottom on the opposite side. I sat still for a minute. Watching and waiting.

When you are hunting, the anticipation always makes you expect movement at any time. If you move ten seconds too early or you cough at the wrong time, you will lose the only opportunity for a kill. That works with men as well. The first to move is usually the first to die. Or lose out on a meal, whichever the circumstance at the time.

I nudged the horse closer to the edge with my rifle half raised but was disappointed with an empty draw. I spotted the trees where I had cut the logs and the piles of wood chips that were half covered with blown snow. There was a row of new tracks in the snow right up the middle of the draw, but when I looked, as far as I could see, all was still.

I wanted to turn right and follow the edge of the rim, but I knew that with the deep covering of snow, one loose rock under hoof could send us to the bottom in a heap. I would have to keep a distance back from the edge and just ride over from time to time for a look into the draw.

Or go to the bottom and ride right up the center.

I chose neither. I rode to the bottom and paused long enough to check the tracks and decide that I wouldn't eat skunk either. I didn't really need the tracks to tell what it was because when I got to the lower half of the slope, I could smell what it was. No thanks.

I searched the opposite side of the draw and found a relatively safe way up to the top and continued north. The trees on this side were more dense and thicker, and I could only see about forty yards ahead in most spots, so I would have to be more careful in my movements. I would have less warning and less reaction time to act if I spotted game. Or a Lanauxe, for that matter.

The air was still cold, but it felt like the temperature was actually on the warmer side of zero. The small clouds formed by my breath when I exhaled still hung in the air like smoke from a fire.

There was no wind, and the trees stood quiet and tall all around. I could still hear thunder in the distance, but for the moment, the sun shone bright. Ice particles glistened in the morning sunlight on the limbs of the taller fir and spruce trees, and shadows lurked in the spaces below. Occasionally, there was an opening in the canopy that allowed shafts of light to reflect brilliantly off the pure white snow causing the shadows a few yards away to seem even darker.

It was in one of these dark recesses under a huge spruce tree that I spotted movement. It was in the deep shadows under tree, and I couldn't immediately make out what I was seeing.

Sometimes the human mind can't interpret a sight or sound accurately, so it categorizes it into what it assumes that it might be, as in this case. My brain told me that there was a man lying flat on the ground on his back under the low limbs, shaking his head and his feet back and forth. Even though I knew that that was highly unlikely, that is what my brain said.

I dismounted and dropped the reins to the ground so that the roan would know that I wanted him to stand fast. I moved to the left to get some tree trunks between me and whatever was under that tree. There was about twenty yards of ground to cover until I came to the last tree trunk that shielded me from the movement. I needed to get a closer look. If it was man or meat, I needed to be closer for a better shot.

Taking slow, measured steps I eased forward and then turned my body until I was leaning my left shoulder against that trunk. I leaned cautiously around until I had the fir tree in sight. My line of sight was too high now to see under the lowest limb, so I slowly bent my knees and lowered myself down into a crouch.

I could still see the movement, and to my relief, it definitely was not a man. My brain still didn't register what it actually was until I heard the soft cooing that I knew to be a grouse.

There were three grouse hens under the large, sweeping branches scratching the ground where the snow had not accumulated, searching for some small bits of edible plants or small insects that somehow survived in the winter. Or maybe they were digging them up frozen. I couldn't tell.

I could see no way that I would have a chance to get all three. One for sure and likely two, but three was highly questionable.

Now, I consider myself a decent shot and fair to middlin' quick but not in this cold and definitely not with a rifle. Now, if I had me a scattergun, well, it's no use to dream on what ifs.

I leaned my Hawken against the bole of the tree next to me and eased my pistol out of the holster. I took a minute and mentally rehearsed my movements. Should I shoot left, middle, right or go the opposite way and shoot right, middle, left? It seems easier to adjust your aim to the right, so I decided to shoot left first. Left, middle, right.

I actually started thinking of how I was going to cook these birds and how they were going to taste after roasting on the fire. Then I had to stop. My stomach was starting to get in front of my thinking. I took about three seconds and called myself an idiot. "Concentrate," I whispered.

I thumbed back the hammer of my Colt and took careful aim. I waited a second until all three heads were up then shot at the left bird. Instantly, I shifted to the right and shot at the middle one and then the one on the right.

myself against the wall, I leaned my head forward against the rough logs and paused to listen. Nothing but the wind and the ice particles tapping out their winter message on the walls. As I moved toward the door, I could see that the leather strap that served as the bottom door hinge looked like it had been mostly eaten by some small critter. This allowed the door to sag enough to let the opposite corner rest solidly on the threshold. With that and the ice and snow that had blown against the door, I had a time just getting the door open. I would have to remember that if I stayed here any length of time at all. In a bad storm, a body might just get stuck inside if the door wouldn't open.

The cabin smelled of dust and stale air, which to me was still a good sign. It meant that there were no recent inhabitants that might return and lay claim to my refuge and force me back into the cold. I stepped inside out of the wind and struck a match.

I found the cabin to be a snug, one-room affair, about ten feet wide and maybe fifteen feet deep. There was a small, square table and two chairs in the center of the room with an empty flower pot in the middle of the table. There was a shelf about waist high along the left wall, and what few items it held were placed in neat rows like everything had a place.

I blew out the match before it could burn my fingers and tossed it off the porch into the snow. I closed the door and struck another match and lit a candle that I had found

I lifted my head slightly and waited for the powder smoke to lift slowly in the cold air. After a half a minute, I could see that two were still under the tree flopping around—most likely dead, but their bodies just didn't know it yet. The third one had flown into a nearby treetop. I shot again and missed. The bird launched itself into the air with a furious beat of its wings and disappeared behind another spruce tree. I heard it for another few seconds beating a fearful pulse in the air but never got sight of it again.

I looked back under the tree and could still see movement, so I ran forward and went to my knees next to the spruce, ready for a quick shot if it were needed. It was not. The first bird had its head cleanly removed by the .44 slug and was now lying in the snow, slowly kicking one leg in the last throes of death. The second bird still had his head, but the top third of it was missing, and he wasn't moving.

Had there been other folks around—I might have bragged a little about "two out of three and both in the head"—but all I could think of right now was the other meal that flew away.

I slid out my knife and removed the rest of number two's head then tied them together with a piece of rawhide. I walked back to the roan and hung the rawhide string around the saddle horn. Then gathered the reins in my left hand and started to mount when I remembered my pistol. Anyone within about two miles now knew I was here, so I dropped the reins and opened my shooting pouch and began to reload. I put another mark in my personal-disappointment book as I thumbed fresh loads into the pistol. A man could die from not reloading immediately.

When I was finally in my saddle, I took a slow look around to see if I had attracted any attention with all my shooting, but all was still and quiet close up. With a knee, I urged the roan forward and headed east. Moving quietly through the trees, I thought back to the last bird I had eaten just off the trail through the Indian territory after I left Fort Smith.

7

I was about a week out of Fort Smith and had slowed my travels to a leisurely pace and was starting to enjoy the peace and solitude of the area. I was still being mindful of Indians and such, and that by itself is reason enough not to run along full tilt.

With my old Hawken rifle, I had just shot a turkey after crossing the Illinois River. I remember that I was so puffed up and full chested with my eighty-yard shot that I didn't see the old man leaning on the hoe until I had climbed completely out of the draw leading up from the river.

I had been so focused on the bird that I had failed to look around first.

I sat still on my horse for a minute and looked around to see if he was alone. It was then that I noticed a small cabin at the far edge of the clearing.

The old man waved his arm and gestured for me to come on in as he walked toward the downed hen. As I neared, I could see that he was dressed in homespun pants with several patches. His old weather-beaten hat had a tear in the brim and at least three holes in the crown that I could see. His shirt was just a piece of canvas with arm holes and ties on the front instead of buttons. I didn't see a gun anywhere. Not in the open and, as far as I could tell, not in his waistband either.

I pulled up next to him just as he hefted the still-twitching bird from the ground.

He turned toward me and raised the bird about shoulder high and said with a grin, "Four ta five more shots like this here, stranger, and you'll have my whole flock down ta nothin'."

I stared in surprise. "Your flock?" I shook my head in disbelief. "You mean to tell me that that was a tame bird?"

He chuckled. "Yep." He stepped forward and handed me the foot that he had been holding and said, "Well, mebee not rightly tame, but they come get it when I throw the corn out. But we'uns don't aim to let nothin' go ta waste." He extended his right hand. "Hope y'all can stay for a visit, friend. We don't get many that come out this a-way. My name's Nate Childers. What's your'un?"

I switched the bird to my left hand then reached out with my right and gripped his bony, sun-browned fist and replied, "Mine is Tyrel Matthews. Ty to my friends."

"Glad ta know ya, Ty," he said. "Y'all just a-passin' through?"

I nodded and said, "Yes." I was still struck by the fact that I never seen this man standing there when I shot. He had to have been within forty yards of this bird.

I suppose that I was so concentrated on the hen that I failed to look around.

He turned and waved a gesture toward the cabin and said, "Lite and set up to tha house yonder, an Ma will fix up that there feather duster like you ain't never et a'fore. She's fixes a fine stack of vittles, 'specially when we got a visitor to the table."

I thanked him and turned the roan, and he added, "Best tell Ma that you shot this'un away up yonder past tha river so she won't be thinkin' it's one o' hers. I'll be up directly."

I paused and asked, "What about the shot? She would have heard it from there."

He looked up at me, squinted one eye against the sunlight, and smiled. "You shore right 'bout that, Ty. I'm sorry ta be sayin' so, but guess y'all just gonna have ta take yer lumps when ya tell her the truth."

He chuckled again and shook his head as he started walking back to the garden he had been working on. "Whoooweeee, son, I'd be some a'feared ta be standin' in yore boots right about now."

I rode to the cabin and was met at the yard gate by a thin, stalwart, proud woman of close to sixty years. Her brown hair had a touch of gray, and her clothes, while worn over time, were clean and carefully patched. "Welcome, I see y'all done met—I mean have already met Nate. I'm Eleanor."

"Yes, ma'am," I said, "I'm Tyrel Matthews. Most folks call me Ty." I held up the turkey that I had shot. "I'm appears that I shot one of your tame birds by mistake, ma'am. You see, I had just crossed the river and hadn't come up the bank far enough to see the house yet and—"

She laughed. "Is that what he told ya?" She pointed down the field toward her husband. "Don't let that old goat fool you. We ain't had a tame bird on tha place since 'bout a year past when a 'coon got in tha barn and kilt my last two layin' hens." She leaned on the gate with both hands smiling.

"Well, he did say that they weren't exactly tame," I replied, "but they come around when he feeds."

She leaned back and laughed. "So that's why y'all had that scalded dog look on yer face." She waved her hand in front of her face. "Hoohoo, Mr. Ty, Nate done tole you a whopper."

My jaw went slack as I tried to sort out what she was telling me.

"Tha onliest reason he was in tha garden taday was cuz them turkey most always come out ta feed long about this time an' we was needful of some table meat," she said.

She leaned to the side to look around the roan and said with a more serious face, "Y'all see there. Here he comes with his o'le scattergun and a grin from ear ta ear."

I turned and looked over my left shoulder, and sure enough there was the old man with a shotgun in the bend of his right arm and his brown, tobacco-stained teeth showing all the way across his mouth. Well, aside from the two that I could see were missing.

He held up his left hand in a defensive gesture and said with a laugh, "Don't y'all shoot me now, Ty. It ain't ever' day that I can poke fun at a body 'round here other than my Ellie there."

"Come on down from there, Mr. Ty," Eleanor said. "Pass me that bird so's I can get 'er plucked and cleaned fer supper." She looked at her husband and said with feigned sternness, "Quit yer funnin', Nate, and act like you had comp'ny a'fore." Then she straightened and said with a more dignified look. "I'll put coffee on tha boil and younguns stay outta my way for a bit 'til I get this here bird bedded down in tha coals. It'll be a few hours for the cooking of it so be patient."

As she turned and headed around the side of the cabin, Nate said with a continued smile, "I 'pologize, young feller, but that was a hoot if'n I do say so masef." He turned toward a log barn that was hidden from view back in the trees until a body was standing right at the gate. "Foller me yonder, and we'll git a bait o' corn fer yer hoss."

I dismounted and led the horse to the front of the barn where he stopped. Nate pointed to a stall in the rear of the barn that looked as if it hadn't been used in some time.

"Y'all can use that stall there. We ain't had a hoss since our old mare Sally died o' tha festerin' pisen from getting jumped by that sneakin', long-tooth catamount back yonder in the holler." He paused briefly with emotion then added, "I done 'em in right quick with muh scattergun, but the claws done raked deep. I cleaned 'er up best as I ever could an' even used muh pap's mustard seed poultice, but she was done too weak I s'pose."

I stripped the saddle and hung it on the rail then put the roan in the stall. The old man dumped in a healthy dose of corn in the bin as I started to rub down the roan with an old sack.

I heard the bucket thump as Nate set it on the floor, and he said, "I ain't got no call ta ask it of ya, Ty, with this bein' yore own hoss an' all, but would ya mind if'n I rubbed 'im down a mite? I shore do miss tha doin of it."

"Sure thing, Nate, I don't mind at all," I said, handing him the rolled up sack. "If I had only known, I just sold my extra horse yesterday at Fort Smith. I could have sold him to you and your wife just as well."

"Aww," he said sheepishly, "we cain't 'ford no hoss nohow, Ty. I juss miss tha smell an' workin' with a good, powerful animal. 'Lmost like an extree friend most times." He was silent for a spell as he rubbed long strokes down the back and flanks of the tired horse. I suppose the roan had no objections because, as usual, he just stuck his nose back in the feed bin and stamped at a fly occasionally.

After a few minutes of silent work, Nate asked in a quiet, more serious tone, "Ty, are y'all runnin from some fellers?" He paused and laid his arms across the roan's back. "Ya aint got ta say if'n don't wanna. I juss gotta tell ya that they was some fellers by here a couple days back. Mean-lookin' sorts too, they was. Had yer look likes down purty good and was askin' of ya. So I'm needin ta know if you got the law after you 'cause I ain't goin agin no law."

"Yeah, Nate, they're looking for me but not because I've broken any law. And they ain't lawmen either. Those are some mighty bad men where they come from, but I'm not sure how high they will stack compared to regular folks," I responded.

He raised his right hand in a gesture for me to stop. and said "I don't need no 'splainin lessen y'all juss wanna give it, but tha thang is, Ty, I gotta keep my Ellie safe, an' if that means sendin a good man packin, I will." He trailed off.

"Well, Nate, I understand, and I don't mean to bring no trouble to you or your wife." I stared at the loose hay on the ground at my feet.

So they are ahead of me, I thought. I had slowed down my running, hoping they had lost my trail, but not only were they close, they had figured out where I was headed and somehow had gotten past me. It wouldn't take long for them to realize it and come back this way or just hole up somewhere ahead and wait for me to ride to them. I surely didn't want them to come back here and find out that the Childers had warned me or even talked to me. The Lanauxes would have to assume that Nate knew me or, at least, would know the direction I was heading and would not be safe either way. And Ellie, I didn't want to even think about what they would have in store for her.

I made my decision and said, "I'll saddle up and ride out as soon as my horse finishes this corn. I don't want to see you or family come to any harm."

He turned his head toward me and said, "Now, Ty, that ain't my meanin'. We ain't afeared of a pack of long-branded, no-account skunks. Me an Ellie have fit off Indians, drought, grasshoppers, thieves, and land-grabbers, and I ain't about ta be backin up fer no yella-bellied tinhorns." He put an old, bony hand on my shoulder. "No, sir. Y'all stay as long as you be of mind to. I juss had ta ask fer my own self. We'uns here have always been ready fer trouble when it comes, but I'm on tha side of tha law too. I was raised Quaker like, but I've seen enough meanness in the world to know we all cain't just stand by and keep aturn' the second cheek at 'em."

I looked at him and said, "If they come back, then it most likely will be trouble." I shook my head in disgust. "I should have went back and killed those two, but I never have been any kind of hand at fighting."

"Don't you worry none. 'Long as you'uns ain't goin agin the law, then y'all juss stay on here if'n you got a mind to. Like I say, I juss had ta know."

"Well," I said with all the seriousness I could muster, "I did go to all the trouble of shooting that turkey, and I can't rightly just ride off without eating my fair share."

He turned back to latch the stall door and replied, "No. I 'spect not. Juss wouldn't be right neighborly t'all."

We talked the afternoon away while I helped him with a few chores that needed an extra hand. I turned the grindstone while he sharpened up his froe, adz, and two-bit ax. Then we fitted in a new plow beam that he already had shaped out and readjusted the landside and heel so that it fit snugly against the frog and got his plow back in working order. I was coming to genuinely like the old man even more than I had on my first impression.

When evening found us, we had just finished replacing a busted spoke in his wagon wheel and fitted it back on the buckboard. "I feel right shameful about wastin' time on this here wagon when I ain't got no hoss ta pull it. An tha plow too, far as that goes," he explained. "But I'm thinkin' mebee it'll fetch the price of some supplies from them that could use a good wagon."

I stood and stretched my back and said, "Sounds right to me, Nate. No sense in throwing away what could be sold for cash or traded. Or it could be that you might come across a good horse or an ox at a good price."

It was about that time that we heard the jangle of the dinner bell. We gathered up the tools and put them away then headed to the wash basin on the porch to wash away the dirt we had gathered from our day's work. As we approached the cabin, I could smell the rich aromas of supper floating through the air.

I recalled that Mrs. Ellie—as I came to call her—was every bit the good cook that Nate claimed her to be. I had never tasted any turkey with that much juice and flavor. And I'll swear, till my dying day, you've never had a real sweet potato pie until you've tasted hers.

My thoughts were pulled out of the past when the roan stepped off into a hole in deep snow and stumbled. I had to grab a swift hold on the horn to stay mounted.

8

That line of thinking about Mrs. Ellie's cooking almost had me dreading cooking these two snow chickens. With no grease, I would just have to roast it over the fire or pack them in mud and bury them in the coals. No salt, no spices, no grease. And I wasn't sure if I could thaw out the dirt enough to make mud now anyways.

I shook myself out of my reverie again when the roan stopped in the trail for a large tree that had blown over in the wind. I still had my Hawken out ready for what may come, but with my mind lost in the past, I hadn't been studying my surroundings. I pulled the reins to the left, and we skirted the log and continued on.

I figured I was about a mile and a half north and two shades west of the cabin, and the plan was to make a sweeping curve to the east, past the cabin, then south, and come back to the cabin from the east side, which I had yet to explore. I would let the roan work on some hay in the barn while I worked on preparing a quick meal. At least at the time, I figured that was the plan.

I found out the hard way that you can never predict how even a simple task like riding back to the cabin would turn out.

Well, here I am getting ahead of my story.

The thunder continued to rumble, but it was definitely closer now. There was no wind yet, but the clouds were growing across the sky as thick as thistles in a hay meadow. As I said before, we were headed east scouting and looking the country over. I was still hoping for a deer or an elk maybe, and I kept my old front stuffer across my saddle and ready for business.

It's hard to tell, when you are walking or riding, just how much the ground rises under you until you look behind you. We had gone a mite over a mile east, and by the look, we had risen six or seven hundred feet. The snow here was still about two to three feet deep in the open places, but I was able to pick a path through the trees where most of the snow was still on the branches above. The roan had stopped at the edge of a long clearing that ran from up the hill above me to my left and almost straight down the hill to the right. I could tell that the snow was deeper in the clearing, and I thought that was why my boneheaded, stubborn nag of a horse wouldn't go across.

Let me put this in right here for all you would-be cow nurses and lone travelers and explorers: If you are riding a horse that normally acts sensible and does right most of the time, then don't be a bone-headed, stubborn nag of a rider like I was. Trust your horse when he's trying to tell you something.

Anyways, like I said, the roan didn't want to cross, so I kicked and prodded and circled a few times. I coaxed and talked and begged and cussed. And he finally went.

It was about fifty feet across, and when we started out, the snow was about two or two and a half feet deep. We had made it about a third of the way across when the snow got deeper. It was close to four feet, and we were struggling. I hung on as the roan jumped and hopped to keep going like I asked him to do.

Then I heard thunder again. It was right close on top of this mountain. I instinctively looked up to see where the lightning had hit when I realized I never heard the sizzle, crack, and boom of lightning. What I did see turned my guts to jelly.

In the flash of a single second, I realized three facts at once: my horse was right, I was going to die, and the reason there was a clearing from the top of the mountain straight down to the bottom was because of an avalanche just like the one that was going to swallow me in two seconds.

It hit with the force of a loaded steam engine. The first wave of snow came from below our feet, pushing upward. As the avalanche came down, it forced the snow ahead it to move first almost like a flooding river that rises four feet in two seconds. Then the second wave hit, and I was jerked from the saddle. I threw my rifle free and crossed my arms in front of my face and doubled over at the waist, I think. At least that's what I tried to do.

At first, I had the sensation of my horse actually on my back instead of the other way around, but I can't say for sure. I tumbled and gasped for air and tumbled some more. I remember thinking about all those rocks and trees that usually make up a mountainside. Then I didn't think anymore for some time because I was hit with a wicked blow on the right side of my head.

When I opened my eyes, I couldn't see anything. I mean, I could see dim light, but I couldn't make out anything. My left arm was pinned behind me, but my right arm was across my chest, so I moved it slowly to my face. When I rubbed my hand over my eyes, I removed a handful of snow that had been packed over my face.

I looked around in the fading light of the day and saw that my legs and most of my upper body was buried in a huge pile of snow. I was lying on my left side, and the only thing visible above the snow was my head, my right arm, and down my right side to about my third rib.

I closed my eyes against the throbbing pain in my head and listened. I heard thunder again. This time, it was real thunder, and it started snowing big, white, fluffy, puffballs of snow and thousands of them.

The slide had played out near the base of the slope in some ragged trees that had been knocked askew from the earlier avalanches. I methodically tested each muscle and joint as much as possible while being half buried, and, while each one hurt some, I was somewhat relieved to find that nothing appeared to be broken.

With my right hand, I started digging. First, I dug out some space in front of my chest then uncovered down to my waist on my right side. Then I placed my right hand across my chest next to my left shoulder and slowly lifted myself enough to move my left arm. It seemed to be numb, and it felt like pulling a large stick out of the snow. I leaned back, and with some helpful tugs from my right arm, I was able to free my left arm from the weight of the snow.

My whole left arm began to tingle and burn. I've heard that it's like a thousand needles all at once and that might be a close comparison, but I'm thinking more like a thousand rats chewing and gnawing on your exposed flesh.

After ten seconds of the rats, I started to realize that someone had just put my left hand in a bed of red-hot coals. It hurt so much that the world went wavy, and I almost passed out.

When everything came back into focus, I lifted my left hand and placed it in my right. I winced in pain and gasped for breath as I pulled off my left glove and gingerly lifted my hand for inspection. The smallest finger was being unsociable and wasn't standing next to the others. He was hanging off to the side at an odd angle and bouncing with every heartbeat—throbbing, I mean—and every time my finger throbbed, it made my head pound. I dreaded it, but I needed to fix it real quick before it started to swell up. I figured the only reason it wasn't swollen now was because I had been laying on it restricting the blood.

I bit my lower lip and grabbed the injured finger with my right hand and pulled it. I heard the joint pop and felt it straighten next to the others.

I ain't ashamed to say, I bit hard on my lip and whimpered a few times. My eyes blurred with a few tears, and my breath came in ragged gasps for about ten seconds. Son, that hurt.

I leaned my head back and blew out a couple of deep breaths and calmed myself a bit. There's no way to figure out how to get out of this whole situation at once, so I decided to tackle each problem one at a time then move on to the next. I just hoped that one of the problems wasn't hiding in the woods fixing to shoot at me before I was ready to turn my attention to it.

I slowly pushed myself up and dug the snow from around my legs. The first thing I noticed was my empty holster. I dug some more snow, and I was able to wriggle my legs around and pull them free one at a time. I rolled my body to the right down the slight incline until I was facedown in the snow. From there, I bent my knees and pushed myself up with my right hand to a standing position. I staggered like a drunk miner for a bit then steadied myself against a tree and paused to take stock of my situation.

I hurt everywhere, and it took me a minute to focus my thoughts. It even hurt to think.

I leaned my head against the tree and took a few deep breaths in the cold, crisp air. I brought my thinking back to the immediate situation that I was in to figure out my best move from here. I had no horse, no gun, and no supplies. It was late afternoon, and I knew I wouldn't make it to the cabin before dark without my horse.

I looked around for horse tracks, but I couldn't see any sign of him through the heavy snow. It was only about thirty yards through the trees to the bottom of the slope, and I figured that's where he would head to if he was able, so I decided to do the same. I was caught by the realization that he may be buried under tons of snow, and that hit me hard right in the center where I lived. I had to keep the hope that he was alive and ahead of me. That was all I could accept at this point.

I pushed off the tree and took a step down the slope and suddenly realized that I was in much worse shape than I originally thought because I fell flat on my face. I landed in the snow, which cushioned the blow somewhat, but it was like getting hit again all over the body. I screamed. I know I did.

My right hip was bruised and tender, and when I stepped out with my right leg, it let me know in a hurry. I rolled to my side and crawled to my feet again. Trying not to put too much weight on my right leg, I limped and shuffled down the slope to the bottom and eased down to the ground with my back against a large tree. It was cold and getting colder, but I was sweating.

I tried to consider what I knew. The cabin was approximately a mile to the southwest, maybe a little less, and if I could walk with any speed at all, I should be able to make it there in two to three hours even with the deep snow and difficult terrain. If I couldn't walk with any speed at all, then I was stuck, and I would have to survive the night with what I had in my pockets.

My best bet for survival was to get up and walk, so I got up. I took a bearing on an old dead snag about one hundred yards distant in the right direction then surveyed the ground around me for the best path. Then with great reservation, I took the first step toward what I hoped was, eventually, shelter. I just wished that I knew how many steps were left to go before I got there, or if I would get there at all.

I paused several times to rest and replan my steps, but I finally made it to the old tree. I was sweating profusely, and I realized that my jaws hurt from continually clenching my teeth against the stabs of pain that came from my various injuries. I leaned my head against the peeling bark and blew out a long, ragged breath and tried to convince myself that I could and would keep going. I was thankful that I even survived and did take a measure of confidence from the fact that I had reached my first goal—this tree—even as short as it was. As gratifying as that was, I also realized that I had only covered the first hundred yards in the total distance of over seventeen hundred yards that made up the mile I had to travel.

"Son, if you don't at least try, you'll never do," I heard echo in my thoughts.

Over the next hour, I had set shorter and shorter goals until I was now driving simply from tree to tree. The wind had come in to join the heavy snowfall, and it had grown almost completely dark. I still had the feeling that I was heading in the right direction because I knew that all run-offs eventually led to a stream then a river, and I should be right close to the stream that went by the cabin.

My hip was doing some better, but my head felt like it was under a herd of buffalo running all out. I probably needed water and I know I desperately needed sleep, but neither one would happen tonight if I didn't get to the cabin. I had always been told, "Don't eat snow to get your water unless you're sitting in front of a fire. Without the heat, you could freeze."

There was a low depression in the snow in front of me about three feet deep, and I didn't want to go through it, so I moved to the left to skirt around it. I had to move even further to the left so I wouldn't have to cross an old tree that had fallen sometime in the past. It was that move that caused me to find the tracks of a horse. My horse, I hoped.

The fact that we had both been funneled to this spot by obstacles was most likely the only reason I had found the trail.

With renewed vigor and excitement, I set out to follow the alternating depressions of the tracks before they could fill with snow. I had to assume that they were the tracks of the roan because I hadn't seen any sign of others horses in the area. and these were of a shod horse. Then I had a sudden thought. If I just followed the horse tracks, I might not find my way to the cabin. I decided to gamble on the horse, and, who knows, maybe the horse was heading to the cabin.

I paused to study the area around me as far as I could see in the darkness. I turned to look over my shoulder, and my left hand bumped against a nearby tree and the pain flashed brightly behind my eyes and sent me to my knees. I cradled my left hand in my right and held still for a minute until the stars dimmed in my vision. I couldn't do anything for it here in the dark, so I stood and with a deep sigh. And what seemed to be the last dredges of my strength, I started walking again.

By the tracks, if it was actually my horse, he seemed to be moving okay, and I hadn't seen any blood on the snow.

I labored on through the deep, swirling snow, occasionally having to pause to verify the direction of trail so I didn't get lost. The snow had just about covered the tracks to the point that I couldn't make them out when I crossed another trail.

These tracks were fresh. They were made only moments ago, and they were small. Much smaller than a horse. I'd bet they were wolf tracks, but it was hard to tell with all the loose, new snow everywhere.

I peered into the darkness, but I couldn't make out anything aside from the vague outline of the print. Now, I don't know about you, but I ain't in no ways comfortable meeting a wolf in the woods in the dark. No matter how you spin that situation, that's bad news.

I took a notion of the direction the horse was moving and set off into the night trying to hold a straight line of travel. The trail was nearly invisible under the accumulating snow and the low light conditions. I would have to trust my instincts now.

I was so cold and tired that I was having trouble focusing my thoughts. I had used up all my strength and will to survive and kept moving now because I was just too ignorant to know that I had failed.

I stumbled and crawled on and on until that's all I knew. One more step. One more tree. One more foot gained.

I had stumbled into a clearing and was moving to my left to get around a huge rock. I reached the corner of the rock in the drifting snow and stepped around it. That's when it finally dawned on me that rocks don't have corners. When my eyes focused clearer, I was looking at a porch with a wood pile and a door. I couldn't get my frozen mind to grasp how I managed to make it here in one piece.

With numb fingers, I pulled the latch string and got the door open and fell inside. I climbed to my knees and closed the door behind me then crawled to the stove. It was cold in the cabin but not even close to the cold I had just came from.

I collapsed and lay still on the floor with my eyes closed. I couldn't begin to understand how I had survived or how I had made it back to the relative safety of the cabin. Blind luck mostly, I guess. Some may call it a survival instinct. I don't care, call it what you want, it worked for me this time.

I was startled awake by the throbbing pain in my hand and realized that I was still on the floor. I had to forcefully will myself to get up. Through some unimaginable depth of self-preservation, I had made it this far, and I would not let myself quit now.

When I opened the stove, I could see a few small coals laying in a row in the ashes where they had once been a log. I reached into the wood bin and forced my cold fingers to bend around a handful of wood chips and slivers that I had picked up after chopping the firewood. When I reached in and lightly sprinkled them on the coals, the heat from within felt like a furnace on my stiff, nearly frozen hand. I prayed with every long breath as I blew on the embers that I would not fail here. I waited briefly and blew again.

Through the tiny, swirling tendrils of smoke, I saw the small wood chips begin to glow. I forced myself to wait until the smoldering chips actually produced a flame before I added more wood. It didn't take long for the hungry fire to grow into a steady heat source. I slowly added larger chunks.

When the wood began to pop and crackle in the heat of the flame, I filled the stove and crawled to the bunk. I took off my wet clothes and rolled up in the blankets with my teeth chattering and closed my eyes. As I slowly began to warm, I remembered thinking that I never found my horse, and then the world went dark as exhaustion finally won the battle.

When I finally opened my eyes again, it was well into the afternoon, and I felt like I had been dragged down the tracks behind a steam engine. My mouth tasted like a stagnant swamp bog, and the nerves in my fingers and toes still burned from the first stages of frostbite. When I tried to move to stretch the soreness from my muscles, they seemed to all cramp and draw into knots at the same time.

I looked at my left hand and could see that it was swollen badly and was dark purple and blue around the joints of my little finger. I flexed it slowly and winced in pain, but at least I could still move it.

I forced myself to sit up on the edge of the bed and slowly stretched the muscles until they surrendered and began to relax. I moved from the bed to a chair in front of the stove and kept the blanket wrapped around my shoulders to help retain some warmth as I set about coaxing the fire back to life once again. I was hungry, but I didn't have the energy or the motivation to cook and wasn't at all sure there was anything left to cook except filet of boot or rawhide soup. That's when I remembered how excited I had been about the grouse and how disappointed I would be if I hadn't just escaped death once more.

With the fire growing steadily, I tried to recall all the events directly after the slide and was only becoming aware of a few bits and pieces when I remembered the roan again. I needed that horse. Without him, I would be limited to traveling within a mile of the cabin in any direction and even less in bad conditions. With the horse, I could easily go ten miles and be back just after noon. I would need all the range I could get for hunting.

I needed to hang my clothes next to the stove to dry, so I leaned forward to pick them up when a severe cramp gripped my back. It hit me so fast that I couldn't stop my forward momentum and fell against the stove then rolled to the floor and landed on my side. I teared up again and bit my lower lip to stifle a scream. To my relief, the stove was only warm and hadn't become hot enough to burn me on top of everything else I was dealing with.

I gasped in pain and alternated between moaning and holding my breath as I tried to find a position that would ease the spasm. Thankfully, it finally gave up on its own volition and released me.

I was breathing hard and drew in several gulping, ragged gasps. I lay there on the floor and began to feel sorry for myself with everything that had happened to me in the last two weeks.

I worked my way back into the chair and pulled the blanket back around me. I kept the door of the stove open to provide more draft for the flames and carefully hung my clothes on the back of the other chair. Then I positioned it near the stove in hopes that they would dry quicker.

I needed to go out and find the roan, but it would be a death sentence to go out in wet clothes. I began to take stock in my current situation and realized again that I now had no gun. When I was hit by the wave of snow, I had lost my grip on the Hawken. No. I had thrown it so it didn't come back and hit me, and somewhere in the tumble down the hill I had lost my pistol as well.

How can a body be encouraged by that? Here I was smack in the middle of God's creation, in the depths of the winter with no horse, no gun, and no food.

Then I got mad. Mad at myself. I couldn't be mad at the situation. I couldn't be mad at the weather or the avalanche. No, sir, it was all on me. I could stay here and sulk like a whipped dog or I could lick clean the wounds of fate and meet the next problem standing on my feet.

I hoped fate wouldn't mind if I was kind of stooped over and gimping along. At least, I would be on my feet. Mentally, anyway.

I melted some snow in a skillet and drank the first water I had in nearly twenty-four hours. It seemed to help some, so I did it again. After thirty minutes, most of the moisture had been forced to evaporate from my clothes and the cabin was warming up, so I slowly, gingerly began to dress. I could barely raise my left arm. My boots had taken the longest to dry and was the last thing that I put on aside from my coat and scarf.

It was already late in the day, and it would be dark in just over an hour. Two at the most. So I closed the stove door after filling it with wood and forced myself to get moving. I went out onto the porch and closed the cabin door tight against the cold and kicked my way through the new snowfall to the barn. I still hurt with every step, but I had to keep pushing myself. The barn door was still closed, and there were no new tracks around the front or sides since the snow had stopped. I raked back some of the snow that had piled in front of the door and swung it open enough to get inside.

I found exactly what I expected. Everything was just as I had left it. I opened the stall door and forked some hay into the manger and pushed the front door open another two feet. At least if the roan came back on his own, he could get in and have something to eat.

I headed down the trail toward the first water hole that I had cut into the ice, searching for tracks along the way. I would look there first, figuring that if the roan didn't come back to the barn, then he would, at least, be looking for a drink. Then I would go upstream to the second hole and check the snares for something to eat.

When I arrived at the now-frozen hole, I found two sets of deer tracks crossing the ice-covered water, but with no long-range weapon, they were of little interest to me right now. There were no other tracks around since the snowfall last night, so I moved north following the stream to the second hole.

As I knew it would be, this one was frozen as well. The difference was that there were several sets of tracks from the trail, to the hole in the ice, and back. The most exciting thing for me to see was that the roan had been here. I could see the clear outline of his shod hoofprint, so I knew it was him. He had come back several times, and I could see that he had done his best to paw through the ice for a drink. There were also tracks of the wolf and a single set from a lynx or a small cougar. That made me look around quickly. I saw no movement.

I was thirsty, and my head was pounding again, but I had no tools to open the ice, so I turned my attention back to tracking my horse.

I followed the trail up into the trees for about a hundred yards, but then the tracks changed. The story that I read in the snow was that the roan had given up on a drink and had come back this way on the trail and was right here when the lynx came along. When the roan caught the scent, he bolted into the trees to the north.

I hoped that he didn't go far because the light was fading fast and the moon wouldn't be visible until around midnight. And that would depend on the cloud cover at the time.

I had gone close to a quarter of a mile when, to my great fortune, I spotted the roan. One trailing end of the reins had gotten twisted on a limb when he had jumped an old snag while trying to get away from what he thought was pursuing danger.

He pranced nervously and pulled at the reins as I got closer. I spoke to him in low, soothing tones, and I apologized. Then I asked for his understanding of why an ignorant cow nurse would get the fool notion that he was the smarter of the pair between horse and man. I said, "The next time I won't question you. I promise."

The saddle was hanging off to the side most likely from being tossed around in the slide. I saw no signs of the two grouse or my rope that had hung next to the horn, and one pocket of my saddlebag was torn open and empty. So much for my old flintlock pistol that Josh had urged me to keep.

Even though the ax-head had been covered with a stout leather sheath while tied to the saddle, it had still been twisted around so hard that it had cut through the sheath, and the back skirt of the saddle. But it was still there.

The roan was shaking as I patted him and looked him over and continued to ask him questions, but he must have been upset because he wouldn't talk to me. He just rolled his eyes and stood on splayed legs.

He flinched and sidestepped when I released the latigo and pulled the saddle free to check for cuts and injuries. He looked fit and felt sound as far as I could tell. The ax had only cut a small scratch on his back, so I cinched the saddle back in place. I freed the reins and led him back toward the snare line. He was so tuckered out that I didn't want to ride unless I had to.

Now, I have gone twenty-four hours before with no food several times, and a few times I have even had to go three days, but in this cold, with all I've had to go through, I desperately needed nourishment.

By the time we got back to the trail, the roan had stopped sidestepping at every shadow and finally began to trust me again. He must have been just as sore as I was, and I would have to remember that in the coming days or so, we both would have time to recover.

We made it back to the stream, and I used the ax to open the ice, and we both drank our fill. When I stood up, I actually felt waterlogged, but I knew that my body would absorb it all within the next hour or so.

We made our way back to the barn, and after I spent the last of the dying light tending to the horse, I went to the cabin for another cold and hungry night.

The next morning, I awoke early but simply lay there in my bunk after I added fuel to the fire. I had a mountain of stuff to do, but my attitude was working against me. I would have to work hard to keep self-pity down and my survival instinct at a peak.

First thing's first: I needed to keep working on improving my wood supply and I needed food. As long as I had fire, I could melt snow and minimize my trips to the stream. I was too stiff and sore to use the ax safely and efficiently right now, so I decided to concentrate on food.

I pulled back the blankets and began to dress for the day. I figured that once it got moving that my mind and body would fall into the routine and I could keep going.

We finally headed into the trees toward the snares. The roan was bone weary and I wasn't much better, but some things just had to be done, and I wasn't about to leave him here to get fat on hay when he could be helping me find a fat deer. I told him we would just take it slow and he could stop when he needed.

The first three snares hadn't been touched. Not even a new track. But I had a rabbit in the fourth one. It was a spring snare, and the rabbit was six feet above the ground hanging by one back leg. The fact that it was hanging so high was the only reason it was still there. When I rode up, there must have been a hundred prints in the snow where the lynx had been jumping and pacing trying to grab the frozen body hanging above. He must have gotten real close because the rabbit was missing a front leg and there were blood smears in the snow where it had been eaten.

Maybe it was a bobcat instead. It seemed to me that six feet wouldn't be much of a jump for any kind of lynx unless he was young and small. Or maybe injured. I'd have to remember that. An injured animal will sometimes attack in defense when it thinks it can't run away.

It made little difference to me at the time because I now had supper. Since the carcass was frozen and I had lost game from the saddle before, I put the rabbit inside my coat pocket where it couldn't fall out for any reason.

I decided not to check the last four snares right now because the roan needed some rest and my stomach was beginning to wonder if my neck was still attached. We went south along the stream and stopped at the hole in the ice for both of us to drink again before we headed back for a much-needed rest and, finally, some food. I was worn to a frazzle, but the roan had stumbled once on the trail from sheer exhaustion so I elected to lead him back to the barn when we left the stream. And I let him take his time.

Not that I felt sorry for him you see. I just didn't want the fool to fall on me and break my leg. Sorry old cuss anyway I thought but maybe now I was just trying to cover how bad I felt because all this was really my fault.

After we entered the barn I stripped off the saddle and bridle then rubbed him down good taking care to look for any injuries that I may have missed earlier. He stood still in the stall and only ate two mouthfuls of hay then hung his head and dozed while I worked on him with the sack cloth. I methodically checked each leg, from belly to hoof, for any cuts, bruises, lumps, bumps, and anything else out of the ordinary.

All was well that I could see. "You an' me got pretty lucky yesterday," I said. He twitched his ears but didn't respond. I suppose he had the right to be still mad at me.

I closed the door of the stall then the door of the barn and stumbled through the snow to the cabin.

When I laid the rabbit on the table, I was feeling pretty good knowing that this food wasn't going to get away this time. Well, you know, feeling as good as a body can feel that's been run over by a snow train, starved out, frozen out, and lost in a blizzard.

With no grease for a skillet and a wild rabbit in the winter not having much fat, I decided to roast small pieces of meat over the fire. Even without salt and grease, I was amazed that a wild rabbit could taste that good.

With some food finally pushing at the back of my belt, a warm fire going at my feet, and my horse in the barn, I was feeling sort of pleased. Ain't it curious how little it takes to be content sometimes? I could name a whole passel of things that would make it better, but right then, I had all I needed. Except a week's worth of sleep.

With that, I stoked the fire and closed the stove door then curled up under my blankets and slept.

A few hours later, I stood to my feet and stretched. I felt some better, but all the soreness was still there. I figured I couldn't do anything from here except get better unless I tried to ride another snow slide, and that was not on my list of things to get done.

I donned my coat and gloves then went to see if I could convince my old Cayuse to go for a walk. When I walked into the barn, I saw the roan's head come up. He had been dozing, and by the slow movements he made I could tell he was just as sore and tired as I was. He had plenty of hay in the bin, but by the look of it, he hadn't eaten much.

I still had some rabbit left and I could use the rest too, so I went back to the cabin with the wooden bucket full of snow. After placing the skillet on the stove, I scooped handfuls of snow into it. When that was melted, I poured it back into the bucket. I brought in more snow to melt until I had a bucket full of water.

I went to the barn and let the roan drink. It was somewhat over a gallon and maybe closer to two, but that old horse only drank about half of it then just stood there.

I know, he was just acting all stove up to get me to feel sorry for him. And it almost worked, but I caught myself in time. Just to show him that I knew he was funnin' me, I decided to give him another rubdown with the sack and a scratch of two between the ears.

I closed up the barn leaving the bucket inside the stall in case the roan got thirsty before the water froze. When I went into the cabin, I carried an armload of wood for the night even though there was still plenty of daylight left. I was tuckered and didn't even care who knew it. I sat down at the table and finished off the remains of the rabbit then collapsed into the bunk.

I awakened several times in the night to readjust for a cramp or a bruise that I was laying on. Once, I even bumped my left hand and cried out. That one hurt. It seemed to have shook the sleep right out of me and caused me to lie awake for some time.

9

While I was lying there letting the pain and the throbbing subside, I thought back down the trail to the events after I left Fort Smith. After my current situation, they were almost pleasant memories.

I had traveled up the Arkansas River until it was joined by the Verdigris and Neosho Rivers and stopped at Fort Gibson to set in some new supplies. It was an established settlement and army fort founded in 1824 and was busy with activity. There were keelboats moving along the Arkansas River delivering supplies and goods from Fort Smith and returning from up the Neosho with kegs of salt from the trading post of La Grande Saline. There were canoes bringing trappers and hunters from down the Arkansas and the Verdigris and all points north and west. There were log cabins, shacks, and tents strewn across the plains surrounding the fort, and as I sat my horse on a small hill overlooking the scene, I'd swear that if I was of a mind to, I could count near three hundred folks all from this one spot.

It sort of made a body feel cramped for space. At least in places like New Orleans and Fort Smith, there were all kinds of buildings blocking the view around you, and you couldn't see everybody at once. I was new to this area, but I was already feeling like I was getting squeezed out of the country.

I made a quick ride in to the general store to the east of the fort and purchased a side of bacon, beans, flour, salt, hardtack, dried meat, a new shirt, and a can of peaches. And come to think of it, you may not believe me, but it was that can of peaches that saved my life. Well, the can did, not the peaches.

I left the fort behind and had crossed the Neosho River on a ferry raft. I then struck north toward the far reaches of what the government now calls the Indian territory. It had been known as the Louisiana Territory until it was purchased under the office of Thomas Jefferson in 1803. Known as the Louisiana Purchase, it stretched over eight hundred thousand square miles from the gulf to the interior of Canada. It sort of makes sense that after you buy something, you get to call it a purchase.

As the shadows of evening began to overtake us, I started searching for a quiet spot to hole in for the night. I found a low hollow that had plenty of thick brush and trees around for security. The opening was only about ten feet across and maybe twenty feet long, and I was at the north end with my back against the trees. I staked the roan at the south end, where we had come from, so he would be the first to be alerted if anyone were following us.

After I had cooked some bacon and chewed some hardtack biscuits, I sat back and thoroughly enjoyed the peaches. In fact, I was some disappointed when they were gone.

I reached behind me with my left hand and set the empty can on a shelf of rock where the small hollow started. Later, after having forgotten about the can, I rolled up in my blanket and drifted off to sleep listening to the crickets, frogs, and soft crunching sound of the toan cropping grass less than ten feet away.

A few minutes after midnight while I was sound asleep, there was movement in the brush fifteen feet behind me. A six-foot-long rattlesnake raised its head and tested the air with its forked tongue flicking in and out of its mouth. It slowly crept through the grass drawing closer to the strange heat source that it detected lying on the ground.

Hunting hadn't been productive on this cool night as all the small rodents were holed up seeking shelter. The snake knew that whatever this was in front of him, it was too big to eat, but he could tell it was warm and that was just as good. He wasn't worried about safety either. In the past, he had bitten several objects much bigger than him, and they had all given in to his deadly poison. He decided that he would stretch out next to this warm object and wait for the sun to reappear tomorrow.

I was still in deep sleep, curled snugly in my blankets, and was unaware that death was inching closer with every minute.

The snake came to a point where the grass met a cold rock shelf, and he knew that all he had to do was cross the rock and drop down into the hollow and he would be less than a foot from the warmth he desired. When his head cleared the lower edge of the rock shelf and he started to lower himself into the space beyond, the warm thing in front of him moved. It began to lift and roll over. Instantly, the snake jerked its torso into a tight coil, preparing for a deadly strike. Its body brushed against the empty can causing it to grate against the rock surface and fall over with a metallic thump.

The noise hadn't even finished echoing in the night when I was on my feet with gun in hand. It was too dark to make out any details, but I could hear the distinct rattle of a startled snake in the dark. I stepped back and dropped a handful of dry leaves on the fire and waited until the flame caught and flared brightly.

That's when I saw the biggest, fattest rattlesnake I had ever seen. He was over six feet long, and his girth was bigger around than my doubled-up fist. His buttons were large enough that in the still night air, they sounded like dry gourds shaking in the wind, and there must have been ten or twelve of them.

It was then that I realized the snake had been less than two feet from me when I heard the can move on the rock. My mouth went dry, and I felt an icy shiver start between my shoulders and run down the length of my spine. This was just the feeling that Ma used to describe as "my soul puddling around my feet."

After a tense momentary standoff, the snake turned and retreated into the brush where he presumably had come from. I knew I was not going to get any more sleep here with that monster crawling in the brush, so I decided to move on.

The roan wasn't happy with me when I brushed his hair down and threw the saddle blanket over his back just before one in the morning. He didn't say anything but just turned his head and looked at me with an expression that said, "Are you serious?"

"Judge me if you want to, but I ain't laying back down on the ground here," I said as I hefted the saddle into place. "I don't care if we are walking or standing, but I'm going to be up in this saddle 'til we are clear away from here. That thing could have swallowed my whole leg."

The roan took a deep breath and let out a sort of half neigh and half sigh with his head shaking all the while.

It sounded suspiciously like a laugh to me.

I shook out and rolled my bedroll then tied it in place behind the saddle. After I made sure that there were no hot coals left in the fire, I tossed the remaining pieces of charred wood into the brush. I stirred the ashes and mixed in some dirt then kicked dust over the whole area to conceal the spot as well as I could in the dark. It wouldn't fool anyone for long, but it might stand a passing glance if someone were in a hurry.

I hadn't seen my pursuers in a while, but I had to assume they were still back there, so I would continue to take precautions.

I started to mount then remembered the empty peach can. I eased across the hollow in the dark and stopped at the edge of the shelf. I was almost certain that the snake was gone, but just as sure as I reached down, without knowing, I could lose an arm.

I squatted down and grabbed a handful of sand and threw it in an arc so that it spread out over the whole shelf. If that old forked-tongued devil had still been around, he would have stood up and complained when the shower of sand fell. All remained quiet.

I placed my right hand on the edge of the shelf and leaned forward searching in the dark with my left. I figured that if I had to lose a hand, it should be the left one, so's I would still have a gun hand to stand up and shoot him with.

After a few empty grasps, my hand finally bumped the can, and that grating sound near sent shivers through me again. I grabbed it up quick like and stepped back, still expecting the twelve-pound creature to appear. I had heard them called *Crotalus adamanteus* by a New Orleans professor I once had dinner next to. Me, I just liked to call them *dead and good riddance* most times.

I felt another shudder go through my bones as I bent to bury the empty can in the soft sand next to the roan. That old horse, he just craned his neck back and looked at me like I was from Texas or some such strange place, and he just couldn't figure me out.

I climbed aboard and urged the roan out of the hollow and stopped at the edge of the brush. I waited in the dark, listened to the night for several minutes before moving on. I should say, "I tried to listen." All I could picture was that twenty-foot-long, fifty-pound rascal coming out of the grass at my feet. Well, it looked that big at the time.

I shuddered again.

We had ambled north through the night making better time after the moonrise just after three in the morning. We paused often to listen and to look for the paths of least obstacles in the pale moonlight. Just short of daybreak, we came to a long, slow rise, and I could hear frogs and crickets in the distance. I heard the deep, rumbling baroomp of large bullfrogs and the high-pitched chirping of the smaller tree frogs. As we got closer, I heard the lapping sound of waves and the lonesome call of a night loon, followed by the splash of a fish.

When we crested the rise, I caught the bright reflection of the moon shimmering on the ripples across the surface of a large body of water. The natural wilderness symphony of animals, rodents, and insects went quiet along the near bank in front of me, but I could still hear the calls, splashes, clicks, screeches, and chatters from the far side of the lake. I sat still on the saddle and drew in the familiar smells of fish, mud, rotting vegetation, and the crisp, cool air blowing across the water.

I turned the roan to the right and began skirting the bank along the east side as the first streaks of light filtered over the horizon. I heard another fish jump, and I decided that come hell or high water, I was going to eat me a fish that day. Just thinking about it fairly set my mouth to watering. The problem was that I didn't have any fishing tools so I would just have to make do with what I had.

As the sun peeked over the horizon and began painting the landscape orange and gold, I spotted a small creek dumping into the lake from the east. This would be a good place to make camp and finally cook a decent meal.

Locating a flat, clear spot under some towering oak trees, I made a quick camp and staked the roan in a patch of knee-deep grass that should keep him busy for a few days.

Then I went to work on my fishing gear.

For thousands and thousands of years folks have been catching fish through many different methods. Some used lines and hooks, some used nets and traps, and still others used spears. I was going to use some of those methods as well. I had it in my mind to apply a slightly more hands-on approach. Well, a lot more hands-on to be exact, but first, I needed to get a trap built in case that didn't work.

I started off by gathering plenty of wood for the fire. Then, I cut about thirty slender, straight poles between ten and fifteen feet long from the young trees scattered throughout the area. Then I stripped all the bark off in strips about a half inch wide. I would use these strips of bark as rope so I didn't have to use all of my rawhide. As long as you use it while it's green and flexible, it works great and will dry solid in whatever position you leave it in. Next, I took three of the smaller poles and heated them over the fire and began flexing them each into round hoops of approximately three feet in diameter. When I had a hoop formed, I would overlap the ends and tie them with the bark. Then I made one smaller hoop just big enough to get both my fists through side by side. From the pile of poles, I cut eight sticks about three feet long and tied the ends around the small hoop equal distance apart. Then I tied the other ends of the short poles to one of the large hoops, creating a large funnel shape. I filled the gaps between sticks until I had no openings more than an inch wide.

I then began attaching the long poles around the outside of the large hoop until I had created a tube with the funnel suspended in the center. I used the two remaining large hoops to support and strengthen the tube from the inside about two feet apart. This left about five feet of each pole hanging over the last hoop. I simply pulled these together and tied into a bundle. Once again, I filled the larger gaps between the poles with smaller limbs until I was satisfied that my fish trap was escape proof.

The idea is that a fish will be guided down the short funnel into the larger body of the trap but then not be able to find the small hole to reverse his direction and escape. Now there are several ways that you can use a fish trap. You can place it in fast-moving water and it will funnel the fish into the trap or you can place it in calm water and build a guide fence with limbs or rocks to force the fish into the funnel of your trap or you can bait it. I chose the bait method.

I found a large pinecone then I gathered several bugs, worms, larvae, and even some small plants with tiny new leaves sprouting from the stems. I started smashing the bait into the cracks and crevices of the pinecone. I made sure that all the insects and worms were dead so none of them would wriggle free in the water. I sacrificed a short piece of rawhide and tied the pinecone to the inside wall of the trap as far in as I could reach. This had all taken me just under four hours, but I was ready now to fish.

I carried the trap to the edge of the lake and surveyed the current for a minute. Laying my hat on the ground, I placed my possibles bag and my pistol next it. I took a full five minutes looking around the lake and back in the trees to make sure I was alone before I walked the trap out into the water. I selected a location just outside the eddy that was created by the stream spilling into the lake. Fish will usually hover in the calmer water just out of the eddy and wait for bits of food to be washed by and then dart out to grab it. I hoped that I was providing that meal. They just had to go inside the trap to get it.

After securing the trap in place with two poles pressed deep into the mud, I walked through the eddy to the calm water on the other side. I continued along the bank until I came to a spot where a large tree had grown right on the water's edge.

Now it was time to try the hands-on method that would hopefully yield a quick catch.

The water was about four feet deep here, and over the years, the wave action had created a large undercut bank among the roots of the tree. I felt around under the water with my foot until I found a couple of holes in the mud and roots.

These holes are usually made by fish burrowing into the mud to create a protected nest and lay their eggs.

I held my breath and pulled my self under the water by roots and found the entrance to the first hole. I laid the back of my hand down on the mud and slid it slowly into the depths under the bank as far as I could reach. Then, I slowly lifted my hand to see if there was a fish hanging lazily in the water.

This one seemed to be empty so I retreated and stood up.

Now, some folks might be thinking about snakes at a time like this with my hand way back in a hole in the mud, but if a body knows enough about snakes, you will realize that they wouldn't be in a hole completely submerged in the water. If the hole goes up above the surface level of the water, then it will have an air chamber inside, and that one might have a snake. These were about four feet deep, and I knew they would not have any air in them.

I moved to the next hole and repeated the process as before, but when I lifted my hand I felt the smooth belly of a large fish. With only my fingertips touching the fish, I slid my arm back until my hand was under his mouth. I ran my fingers up the side of his head until I felt the edge of his gills.

This next part sort of happens real quick like and takes a little practice.

A fish sitting still in the water will open and close his mouth to force water across his gills, and when he has his mouth open, he's almost asking to be caught.

I blocked the hole with my head and shoulders and waited until I got the timing right, and, when he opened his mouth, quickly I put a thumb in and then curled my fingers under his gill plate and hung on tight.

The reaction was almost like grabbing a charge of blasting powder under the water while it exploded.

The fish began to fight, literally, for his life. He twisted and flipped, flexed and flopped, but I kept him pushed back into the hole for a few seconds. When he calmed a little to see if he was free, I slid my other hand into the hole and grabbed his other gill.

This had all happened in just over thirty seconds, and I was beginning to run low on air, so I planted my feet and backed up. As my head broke the surface of the water and I blew out a lung full of stale air, the fish exploded with a new fury.

I hadn't laid eyes on him yet, but I was guessing he was around five to six pounds, although at the moment, he felt more like an angry buffalo calf. I held him low in the water with his tail pointing down. I wasn't sure if this would help, but I hoped that if he was in an uncomfortable, unnatural position, he would be less inclined to struggle. It did seem to work.

I took some extra time and readjusted my grip before I tried to raise him to the surface. I had him in my hand, but it would only take an instant for him to flip when I wasn't ready, and I wouldn't be eating fish. At least not this one.

I walked slowly along the bank to a place where I could climb out easily, and I began to inch my way out of the water. Just as I placed my right foot to take the last step at the water's edge, my left foot slipped in the mud. As I began to fall, I thrust both hands forward out of desperation in an effort to throw the fish high on the bank. I fell on my left side in the mud without seeing where the fish landed.

The mud splashed on my face and into my eyes, and my left elbow sank a full three inches into the soft mire. I heaved myself to my knees and quickly wiped and clawed at the mud until I could see out of my right eye. My left eye was dark, gritty, and beginning to sting but ignored this as I lunged up the bank to recapture my hard-fought prize.

I found my quarry just simply lying in the grass gently flipping his tail and flexing his jaws. A sudden feeling of relief washed over me, and I dropped to my knees, heaving from my efforts.

I drew my knife from its sheath and placed to point in the center of the fish's head. Holding the handle with my left hand, I gave the end of the knife a solid tap with my right hand and ended the struggle and suffering. I stood as I replaced the knife in the sheath and walked back into the water and washed myself free of the mud and sand.

When I was mostly clean and my eye was functional, I staggered up the bank and picked up the fish. Then I headed back to camp to start preparing myself a fine meal. I walked into camp and hung my dripping shirt on a limb and began adding wood to the fire. I used mostly small limbs and deadwood so that everything would burn quickly and create a nice, deep bed of coals.

I retrieved my hat, gun, and pouch and then began to clean the fish by removing the head and the entrails then squatted at the edge of the creek and washed the carcass in the fresh, cold water. From a nearby sycamore tree, I gathered a handful of the large, plate-sized leaves and wrapped the fish until it was completely covered. Next, I scooped a handful of mud from the edge of the water and began to cover the leaves. When the fish was completely encased with about an inch of mud, I buried it deep in the coals of the fire.

In about an hour or so I would have the fish I had been craving.

I spread my bedroll in the sun and lay back with my saddle for a pillow. I slept as the warm rays relaxed my tired muscles and dried the moisture from my pants.

Maybe I should have set out another empty peach can, but I was too tired to worry right then.

I stirred at the sound of the roan nickering and stomping his hoof in the dirt. Judging by the sun, it was near to five in the evening, which meant that I had slept for two hours. I sat up and looked toward the roan. He was staring into the trees to the east with his ears up.

I was fairly sure that whatever he sensed or saw was not a human threat or he would have acted differently. No. This was some kind of animal. Most likely a predator due to the way he was stomping and blowing. Much like he would have protected his herd if he had one.

I stood and picked up my rifle and my shirt as I walked to his side. Shifting the rifle from hand to hand, I struggled into my shirt and stared in the direction he was looking. After a few minutes, he lowered his head and began to crop grass again, and I knew that I could take that as a sign that all was well. Whatever it had been had apparently moved on.

I returned to the fire, and with my knife, I dug a blackened, dried mud ball out of the dying coals. Then working with the knife and a stick, even though it wasn't too hot, I positioned the hardened tube of baked clay on a flat rock. With the backside of the knife, I cracked the outer shell of mud and began peeling away the clay. When I had removed all the clay, I unfolded the sycamore leaves, and I was rewarded with the steamy smell of fresh baked fish. It might have cooked a bit too long, but since me and the chef sort of see things the same way, I didn't think it right to complain.

I should have asked the waiter for a bottle of his finest wine to go with such a fine dish, but the only one around was still eating grass yonder, and he was paying me no mind. I decided that coffee would be just as fine so I refilled my cup and set to it. I sat right there with no wine and very poor service from the wait staff and ate every fleck and scrap of meat that I could get from the bones. I got up from my table in the wild frontier lands full and happy, but I refused to leave a tip.

If I'd had a few days or maybe a week, I could have built a smokehouse and dried some fish to take with me, but I knew I was still being pursued, and I knew they wouldn't give up. I decided that I was far enough ahead of pursuit that I could spend the day resting and maybe get an easy meal from my fish trap. So I lay back again in the fading sunlight and dozed.

I was startled awake again by the stamp and blow of the roan. In the fading light of evening, I stood quickly and picked up my rifle. Walking toward the horse I could see that he was looking in the same direction as earlier. With semidarkness causing the shadows deepen, I could see nothing and I sure wasn't going to walk out there to investigate when the advantage wasn't mine.

After a minute or two, I could hear some rustling in the brush in the direction that had held the roan's attention. It was something large, that much I knew. There was no quick scurrying sound but more of a slow lumbering through the brush. I had in mind that it was an elk or black bear or even possibly a lone buffalo. Then I immediately scratched off the elk because I don't think a horse would be spooked by something that in no way would be a predator.

When no further movements sounded, I moved the roan's picket pin to a fresh stand of graze then sat by the fire drinking coffee and nibbling on a piece of hardtack. I was enjoying the solitude and relaxation of the lake even though there were still a few bands of hostile Indians around these parts. I had all but forgotten about my pursuers in the past hours, and I realized then how dangerous that could be.

My eyes were growing heavy, and my thoughts beginning to run together after a long, enjoyable day.

I slipped into my blankets after I banked the fire against the chill of the night. I even allowed myself to start thinking of coming back here and locating a cabin on that low rise to the north when sleep enveloped me.

I stirred in the night and came awake when I realized that the wind was rising and the temperature had fallen at least ten degrees. It wasn't really cold yet, but it was late in the year, and I could expect winter to claim its hold soon enough.

I judged it to be around four o'clock, and I could see no reason to delay the morning so I got up. I stirred the fire and added some wood and pushed the coffeepot closer to the coals. Then I went to check on the roan.

He greeted me with a soft nicker and a nudge with his nose. I scratched between his ears and we talked for a few minutes about our situation. I asked what his opinion was, and by his silence, I took it that he was leaving the thinking up to me. "Okay," I said, "but if you don't like the outcome, you just remember that I asked." I turned and walked back to the fire. "A fine lot of help you are. I'm beginning to think that you are just along for the ride."

He just jerked his head up and looked at me, but he used wisdom and kept his mouth shut.

After a quick cup of coffee with the first hint of morning light, I walked to the stream and washed my face and hands then strolled back to the fire. I poured another cup of coffee and waited for the world around me to come into view with the first rays of sunrise. When the morning was well on its way, I walked to the water's edge and used a limb to drag the fish trap free of its mooring in the lake. When the wood poles cleared the surface of the water, I could see that they were covered with handfuls of moss and looked like they had been underwater for a month.

I dragged and rolled the trap onto the muddy bank and was rewarded by the sound of fish flopping inside of the wooden tube. With my knife, I cut the bark lashings at the tail of the trap and dumped the contents on the ground. One of the fish was about the size of my open hand, but the other one was more like both of my hands held end to end with my fingers overlapping. They both appeared to be some sort of bream or sun perch.

I was now officially excited about breakfast. I looked up quickly to see if the roan was watching because I had no intentions of sharing with him. He was still grazing with his head down.

I left the end of the trap open so that no fish would be stuck and never harvested, and then I threw the trap back into the water. Now, a body might ask why I would do such a fool thing, and, I'll admit, my reasons are purely selfish.

First off, I wanted to leave as little sign as I could and that is a good way to hide some of it. And second, I might come crawling back to this lake hungry or injured, and by leaving it mostly intact, all I had to do was tie the ends together and bait it.

I gathered up my catch and went to the creek to clean them.

Sun perch are a might different that catfish. They have small scales covering their bodies, and these can be scraped off easily enough. Just drag a knife blade edgewise from tail to head and watch them peel loose. When I had all the scales off, I removed the heads and the entrails then washed them in the clear water.

These fish were thin enough that I didn't need to bake them. They would cook just fine roasting over the fire on a stick. And that's just what I did.

After a fine breakfast of roasted fish and hardtack biscuits and scalding, hot coffee, I packed up and my goods and headed north into the seemingly flat country ahead.

Dakota Territory

I was having fond memories of that fresh fish when the cold inside the cabin brought me out of the thoughts of my travels.

I was shivering again, so I got up and quickly refilled the stove and crawled back into the semiwarm bed the moaned and groaned for a few minutes because I was even more sore now that I was beginning to heal. I eventually dozed again as the cabin slowly began to warm as the early morning light crept across the sky.

It was late in the morning when I painfully dragged myself out of bed. I dressed then put on my hat and coat. I slung my gun belt around my hips and buckled it in place. There wasn't much reason for the holster but, my knife sheath was attached to the left side of the gun bel,t and it seemed easier to just leave it there. I checked the stove again then went onto the porch to get more wood, but when I opened the door I realized that I had company.

The wolf was sitting in the snow about ten feet from the tree line.

This was the first time I had gotten a clear, steady look at him. No, it was a her. It was a large female, and I could tell she was mighty thin. She had black ears and face that faded into an almost-solid gray body. The fact that she was so thin made her paws look even bigger. She cocked her head quizzically and licked her cheek with her long tongue as if to say, "This is as far as I'm going. It's your move now." I stepped back inside and retrieved the remains of the rabbit and tossed them a few feet from the porch. She stood and took a step and hesitated and set back down and looked at me.

I spoke softly, throwing a thumb gesture toward the barn. "Come an' get it, girl. I ain't going to eat them parts, and I'm sure that old hoss yonder ain't that hungry either."

We stood like that for a minute, but she never moved, so I picked up an armload of wood and went back inside. I closed the door quietly and dumped the wood by the stove.

Since I had eaten the whole rabbit last night, I went about my morning routine without breakfast. Without breakfast, the routine consisted of stoking the fire, and that was already done, so I headed out to check on the roan.

When I stepped back onto the porch and closed the door of the cabin. The wolf was nowhere in sight, and the remains of the rabbit were gone. I studied the tracks for a minute but couldn't tell where she had disappeared to.

I crossed to the barn, through the now-packed snow, and paused in front of the door. A chill ran down my spine and melted into my boots. I had a strange, eerie feeling that something wasn't right. My scalp was itching because all the hairs were standing on end.

I turned slowly and scanned the tree line while my hand fell helplessly to my empty holster. I desperately needed to get my hands on my guns—any guns for that matter. I felt defenseless and vulnerable, but most of all I felt exposed.

I leaned back against the wall while I searched the trees and tried to blend in as much as possible. I wasn't sure why I was feeling this way, but I never was one to discount my gut feelings.

Yes, sir. There was something out there.

I sensed it more than anything. No, in fact, I could feel it. There was no movement and no tracks, but I'd stake my neck on it.

Come to think of it, that's just what I was doing. I needed to figure out where I wanted to go from here and what I would do in the future.

That would have to wait because today I had to concentrate on surviving.

I slipped into the barn and spoke quietly to the roan. He was standing in the stall with his head down and his eyes closed. He didn't look up until I opened the stall door. I rubbed a hand down his back and watched his muscles twitch and jump. I knew he must be sore and stiff from all he had been through these last two days.

"I'm sorry, boy, but I got us into this, and now it looks like it's going to take both of us to make it out," I said as I rubbed a hand down each leg again. "You and me have been through some scraps and scrapes together, and I know I can count on you to do your part, and you know I'll do my best too."

I turned and lifted the bridle off the rail, and I'd swear I heard him sigh, but he made no fuss as I strapped it on. I brushed down the hair on his back and put the blanket in place then hefted the saddle aboard. I knew he was probably bruised a might around where the girth rides, but there was no other choice but to cinch it down.

I looked through the crack of the partially opened door to make sure no one was in sight. Finally, I led him out of the barn and closed the door, and then we headed toward the stream to water up. I wanted to wait as long as I could to climb into the saddle, but I also needed to know if he was up to carrying me today, so I reluctantly mounted up and started down the trail.

I suddenly pulled the roan to a halt on the trail. I don't know where my mind was, but I had ridden most of the way to the stream before I realized that I was looking at new horse tracks in the snow. I knew these to be different from the roan because this horse wasn't shod.

Now, I know that no white man would be out in this wide, open land hundreds of miles from any town with an unshod horse. This wasn't a wandering horse either. The tracks stayed right in the trail like it was being guided. A wandering horse will often stop to smell the trail, browse for food, or just go here and there. The only thing I could say that was good about these tracks was that there was only one set. So far.

This had to be an Indian scout from a nearby tribe. Probably Sioux if I remembered correctly from what I had heard about this area.

That must be what I had sensed earlier as I came out of the cabin. I was scared now. He had to have seen my tracks and most likely even knew about the cabin. If he came back looking for me or if he went back to his village and brought others back, they would hunt me down. And I was defenseless. I had 100 rounds for a .50-caliber rifle and nearer 200 for the .44-caliber pistol but nothing to shoot them through. I needed a weapon. And I would need to use all my knowledge and wits to keep myself safe.

The roan started edging toward the stream, so I let him go. I kept my eyes on the surrounding timber, and the trail looking for movement and tracks. When we reached the edge of the ice-covered stream, I opened the ice as quickly and quietly as possible and let the roan drink.

I mounted and headed back to the snares in hopes of finding some more food. I was fairly optimistic since I didn't check the last four yesterday and the weather had let up some. I guessed it to be about fifteen degrees today and almost no wind, at least none here in the trees where we were now.

As we got near to where I had set that first drag snare, I could see a confusion of tracks, and I hoped I had caught something. When I got within twenty feet, I could tell that I had caught something and I had been robbed. There were bloody smears on the ground and bits of fur. From the evidence it looked like I had snared a marten, and something had come by and made a meal of it. And there were Lynx tracks all around the snare.

I hoped that every time a snare went off, it wouldn't become like a dinner bell to this lynx. I decided right there that if I couldn't find my guns that I would have to make a spear and eventually a bow and some arrows.

I had no choice but to keep moving to the next snare. Maybe the lynx would be in the next one and I could eat him. *That would be a fine piece of justice*, I thought.

I circled through the trees near the spring snare, and I was suddenly excited to see movement. The tree was bouncing and swaying as an animal pulled on the rawhide string. I skirted around a huge spruce tree for a better look at my prize, and when I was within thirty feet, I pulled up short.

It was the wolf. She stopped struggling when she saw me and the roan and sat down on her haunches in the snow. The tree wasn't large enough to lift her off the ground, but it did keep her right foot held high above her head. I thought it was rather strange that she stopped fighting but maybe she was keeping all her attention on me for a chance to attack.

But of a sudden I didn't think so. She seemed too calm to be dangerous, and she hadn't shown any aggression before this either. I sat in my saddle and watched her for two or three minutes then I spoke softly, "Hi, there, pup. It looks like you tried to rob me just like that old sneakin' lynx."

She sat still and coked her head sideways and whined briefly. Then it dawned on me.

As I dismounted and tied the roan, I said, "I apologize, girl. It looks like this is my fault. I never thought about using that dried meat for bait, and you probably thought that I had left it for you just like last time." I walked forward until I was about ten feet from her and squatted with my elbows resting on my knees. "I'd really like to let you loose, but you're going to have to trust me," I said softly. "I don't mean you no harm, I was just trying to get some food."

I stood, so if she jumped, I could keep my face protected. Then I stepped forward with my hands at my side. She just sat there like she knew what I was trying to do, so I bolstered my gumption and reached for the rawhide string.

She whined once, like maybe it hurt her foot, but still sat still.

When I pulled the tree down, I held it with my left hand and pulled my knife with the right and cut through the string where it was connected to the tree.

She flinched when I let the tree spring back up, but she didn't get up or try to run. I squatted again and said, "Now let's see about that foot."

She whined and pulled her foot back and almost pulled the rawhide out of my hand. I started to pull back on the string, but then I stopped. I laid the string down on the snow and said, "Come on now. I said you was going to have to trust me." I then reached for her foot.

To my surprise, she didn't move when I touched her. The thong had cut into the skin right above her foot, and I knew it was going to hurt to remove it, but it had to be done.

I lifted her foot with my left hand and shook off my right glove and began to work on the loop with my thumbnail. It taken me a minute or so but finally it came off, and I released her leg.

She reached her head down and began to lick the wound around her leg, and I sat there amazed that I was nose to nose with a wild wolf. I knew then that she had to have been raised for a time around folks somewhere. I figured she either ran off or maybe something happened to them folks and she was left alone. It may have been around here, but I have heard of wolves travelling great distances for one reason or another.

After a minute or so, she looked up and whined softly, but when I reached out to touch her she jumped sideways and ran into the trees. I stood and chuckled deeply with genuine humor. I felt good about what just happened. With everything I had against me right now and knowing the struggles that I faced in the future, I had not expected anything to be able to distract me enough to cause a smile. Yet here I was, standing knee-deep in the snow, smiling and laughing like a fool.

I rolled the rawhide into a coil as I walked back to the roan. Dropping the coil into my coat pocket, I untied the reins and mounted. I turned the roan in the direction of the next snare and booted him forward. We hadn't gone more than fifty yards when I looked into the trees and saw the wolf keeping pace with us.

She kept her eyes on us but stayed thirty yards or so distant, and when we approached the next snare she just stopped and sat down to watch.

I had caught another snowshoe rabbit, or hare as some call it. This one was large and would go a long way toward keeping my belt buckle from rubbing my spine.

I removed the rawhide from the frozen animal and reset the drag snare. I could see the tracks of many rabbits and knew that this snare would eventually produce food again. The next two traps were empty, but each time I stopped to check a snare, the wolf would sit in the snow and patiently wait for me to finish, and then we would all be off to the next one.

The last trap was the deadfall I had made with the log, and it was sprung. The log was lying flat on the snow almost like it was before I moved it. From this side of the log, I couldn't tell what was under the snow, but I knew I had caught something because I could see the tip of a tail.

The wolf could smell it too. She had stopped twenty yards away and pranced and jumped back and forth with excitement, and I knew then that I would have to share whatever was in the trap.

I dismounted and tied the roan to a limb and stepped forward to claim my prize. Under the log was a large porcupine, and he was, thankfully, dead. I lifted the log and removed the animal then reset the trap. Without a gun, I would be dependent on what I could catch, and I may have to set several more just to survive.

I decided to use part of the porcupine to bait the deadfall, so I squatted in the snow and drew my knife. With my gloves in place, I carefully skinned the porcupine and set the carcass aside. I rolled the skin inside out so that only the fleshy side was showing and placed it under the suspended log, and then I cut a small piece of meat from the carcass and draped it over the trigger stick. I didn't tie the meat in place and was hoping that it would, at least, bring the potential game in closer so they would find the bloody hide.

When I stood up and looked around, the wolf hadn't moved from her vantage point. I spoke to her like she could understand me and said, "Don't come close to this trap. I know you are hungry, but I don't want you to get hurt again." She cocked her head to the side as I continued. "I'll share what I catch so just be patient." I hope she understood, but I would have to wait and see. If she decided to come back here for the fresh hide, there was nothing I could do to stop her.

I untied the roan and climbed into the saddle. It was still early in the day, but with the roan's condition, I didn't want to push him too far. He had held up better than I expected after all he had been through, and I made sure I told him so.

He must still be mad because he still wouldn't talk to me. In fact, he was silent all the way back to the water hole in the ice. I led him to the hole to drink then let my mind wander back to the first real disagreement we had. Or at least the first time he quit talking to me anyway.

It had been two days after we had left the lake out on the plains where I had caught those fish. We rode north into a series of hills and canyons with several bluffs of limestone thrust high above by some ancient shift in the earth's crust.

I had caught glimpses of movement on our back trail all day long, and once I even saw the flash of sunlight reflected by a rifle barrel or maybe it was a whiskey bottle. Only now they were much closer. I had thought that maybe we could lose them by switching directions from time to time, but it hadn't worked.

We went into a deep, steep-sided canyon that had several smaller canyons emptying into it along its sides. Our trail wound among the maze of fallen boulders that had dislodged from the bluffs above over the years. We needed to find a path to get to the ridge yonder, but I was concerned about turning into a box canyon with no outlet. The first two openings that we passed were covered with logs and almost grown over with weeds and grass. The third, however, showed the promising signs of a game trail leading down its length.

I turned the roan into this draw at a trot and hurried up the trail to the top. We had just crested the ridge when a shot rang out behind me. I never heard the bullet, so I wasn't sure how close it had come.

I reined to the right along the top of the bluff to get directly above them. My intention was to send a hailstorm of lead down on their heads, but to do this we would have to cross a large crack onto a shelf that had separated from the bulk of the mountain. The roan was having nothing to do with it. I kicked and prodded him until he ventured forward, obviously disliking the rocky outcropping where I wanted to be.

With an oath of frustration I finally dismounted when I couldn't urge him closer to the edge.

I could hear the pursuit moving below getting closer, so I leaned over the edge of the rock and fired at the lead rider. I never knew if I scored a hit or not because the whole world began to move and shift under my feet.

The slab of rock we were standing on was nearly twenty feet long and might have weighed that many tons. And it must have been ready to fall already. When I went to the edge of the slab, my weight must have shifted the balance and the rock began to move.

When I looked toward the roan he was trying to scramble backward on the tilting platform. I leaped close to him and took a handful of reins then jumped over the widening gap left by the shifting rock. Everything was moving fast enough by then that when the Roan finally jumped from the slab, he didn't make any forward momentum. He simply jumped and landed in the void where the slab had been.

There was an enormous rumble from below, and terrified screams from horse and man followed by a thick cloud of dust that would most likely take all day to settle. I didn't know who or what was injured in the slide, and I didn't care to stick around to find out.

I hooked a leg over the saddle and held on because the roan would have left me there. He had tried to keep me from venturing onto that rock, but in my haste to get an advantage on my pursuers I had failed to look the situation over. Well, now he was leaving in a hurry, and I don't think he had any intentions of waiting for me. I think now that I understand why.

Thinking back on it, I guess he had a good reason to doubt my intelligence sometimes. But that was nearly a month ago. I think maybe he was just having a hard time letting things go.

I didn't much like thinking back on places where we almost got ourselves killed and, especially, when it was my fault for getting in the scrape in the first place.

After the roan had finished drinking from the stream, I lay down and drank until my teeth hurt. I stood and brushed the snow from my coat and pants, and the wolf stood like she was waiting on me to get out of the way. So I took the reins and started walking toward the cabin. As I led the horse down the trail, I looked over my shoulder and saw the wolf lay on her belly at the edge of the hole and begin to lap greedily.

By the time I got to the barn, the wolf was sitting in the snow at the edge of the trees, quietly watching us. I opened the door and led the roan into the stall where he immediately stopped and hung his head. I hung the two frozen critters from the traps on the stall rail and removed the saddle and bridle then worked for about thirty minutes on a thorough rubdown. I wondered several times if there was anything else I could do to help the horse recover, but my knowledge was limited so I just kept doing what I knew. I finished the rubdown and checked all four shoes and cleaned his hooves. Satisfied that I had done all I could, I took the rabbit and porcupine and headed to the cabin.

The wolf still sat where she had been, just watching me. So I asked her if she had been there the whole time. No response.

I was about to start thinking that I was bad company to be around when she stood and wagged her tail. Now that was better.

"I said I was going to share, but I'm going to make you come and get it. Let's see just how friendly you are," I said as I sat on the edge of the porch. I took the porcupine carcass and tossed it a few feet in front of me. "There you are. If you're hungry, then come get it."

She took a few tentative steps toward the fresh meat and stopped to look at me. She held her stance for about thirty seconds, and then she came forward and sniffed the meat. Unafraid now, she picked up the carcass and trotted back into the trees. I stood and said, "You're welcome," then turned and went through the door.

After roasting another fine meal over the coals in the stove, I went out onto the porch and looked around. There was still plenty of daylight left, and my wood pile was okay for now. The roan was fed and resting, and I had a full stomach. I would like to say I was done for the day, but when you are surviving instead of living, things are never really done. I scanned left then right, but the wolf was nowhere in sight. I searched the trees for movement of either the wolf or my mounted visitor. I had the feeling that for now I was totally alone.

I decided to create my own remedy for the loss of my weapons. I stepped off the porch and walked to the barn to retrieve the ax then headed into the trees in search of a suitable tree that I could use to make a bow.

After an hour of looking and searching, I finally found a blown-down tree that looked like it was fully dried and cured but it hadn't been there long enough to start to rot. I cut a straight length of a limb that was free of knots. It was about six foot long and three inches across and had a nice heft to it. I then made my way back to the cabin.

There was about an hour of daylight left and the weather was calm, so I decided to sit on the porch and start shaping my bow even though it was still below freezing.

With the ax, I split the hardwood stave along its length, creating two separate pieces that could be made into bows. The wide, flat side would be the face of my bow, but it would still need trimmed and scraped. On the other side, I began to chop away the unnecessary wood in large chunks with the ax then switched to the knife for the slower, finer work. In about an hour, as the sun set behind the frozen trees, I had most of the bows shape already defined. I piled the wood chips next to the door for future fire starters and then went inside to the warm glow of the stove.

I filled the stove and lay back on the bunk and contemplated my future. With almost endless possibilities and unanswered questions, I backed up and restarted my thoughts and just concentrated on what would happen tomorrow.

I went down my mental checklist to put a few priorities in line. I had to take care of myself first, but the roan was just as important because without him, I would most likely not survive.

Next would be keeping warm. That would include shelter, firewood, and warm clothes. But I can't forget about defenses. If I could find them at the avalanche site,

I'd have a pistol and a rifle—if they aren't damaged beyond use. But both of those require powder. Dry powder, to be exact. Of that, I have a limited supply that I had left here at the cabin. Maybe enough for twenty-five shots in the old front stuffer. The pistol used them newfangled cartridges, and Josh Nolan had given me nearly a hundred of those when I bought the gun.

The last, but not necessarily the least, of the priorities would be food. I had very little in the way of supplies or stores. With the bow, I should be able to hunt quietly without using up the precious gunpowder—if I could finish it and make a decent bowstring. Then I would have to make arrows and arrowheads. These would be fairly easy but would require a fair amount of time to complete.

It almost sounds hopeless sometimes. I suppose it all depends on how you choose to look at my situation. So far I have forced myself to keep moving, keep trying, and keep plugging along.

Well, there's always the theory that I'm just a simple man and not smart enough to know when to quit.

10

Soon my thoughts went back to the trail herd that I had ran into on my way north from the lake.

I was riding to the north across the flat, wind-swept plains in the knee-high grass when I became aware of sounds in the distance. At first, I couldn't tell what I was hearing, but it soon became apparent by the smell that I was somewhere just south of a large cattle herd crossing the plains on the Santa Fe trail. I rode forward to the top of a rise and was struck speechless momentarily by the sight over a thousand head of beef cows bound westward into Mexico, which, at the time, covered the entire western end of North America.

The cattle were spread out for well over half a mile, and from where I sat, I could see at least five cowboys moving to and fro around the sea of bobbing horns. There wasn't much dust being stirred up by the cattle due to the recent rains, but the heat wave rising from the herd was immediately evident. The chuck wagon was on the far side of the herd from me traveling along the top of the rise among the slow rolling hills. There was also a remuda of about forty horses trailing the wagon.

It didn't take long to be spotted by one of the outriders working the herd along the trail. He cracked a whip over his head, apparently to draw the attention of the others, and rode toward me.

He was riding a beautiful chestnut pony with a white blaze across one eye and a black mane and tail. He stopped about thirty feet away and as he leaned forward, with the whip coiled in his left hand and his left forearm on the horn, his right was resting on his thigh near his holster, he asked, "What can we do for you, stranger?"

The rider himself was an older man with gray hair and sun-browned skin that stretched tight over his gaunt features. He wore a faded blue shirt and tan canvas trousers tucked in the top of some of the tallest boots I had ever seen before. They covered his entire calf all the way up to his knees. His hat was torn and scuffed and obviously stained with many days of sweat and dirt but still did well at shading is face and neck with its extrawide brim.

"Howdy," I said, "I'm just drifting around, and I heard the ruckus up this-a-way and figured I'd have a look." I nudged my horse forward a few steps and continued.

He looked around slowly, and then still maintaining his distance from me, he rode to the top of the rise and looked beyond. He looked back toward me with a squint and asked, "You all alone out here?"

"No," I said, "why do you ask?"

He got a very serious look about himself and asked as he looked around again, "Who's with you? I don't see no one."

I smiled. "I didn't say anyone was with me. You asked if I was alone, and I ain't. You're here. And them others at the herd are here, so I ain't exactly alone out here."

"That's fair," he replied with a still, serious face. "So you're traveling alone? I mean aside from your horse?"

"Yep," I said, "that'd be about right." I kind of liked this odd-looking gent. For some reason, he reminded me of our neighbor back home. Gray headed for one, but maybe it was more the way he looked at you and talked to you, and his eyes and his mind were everywhere around you all at once. You would get the feeling that at any time he could tell you how many ants and dung beetles were within a fifty-foot circle of you. He seemed to take it all in at once.

"Do you think your *segundo* would let me share a cup of coffee?" I asked all the while knowing that if I was accepted at the fire, it would include a meal as well.

"It's about time for Sanders to be locatin' a spot for the cook fire, so let's ride back and see," he replied as he turned his mount in beside me. "I'm not a distrusting man, mister, but I'll let you know on the front side that there will never be less that two guns lookin' at you for the whole time that you're with us. We've had some trouble back down the trail, so we're kind of used to it, if you get the idea."

I said honestly, "I understand. My name's Ty Matthews"—I threw a thumb over my shoulder—"from back yonder and headed nowhere but your fire."

"Mine's Jessup. My front name's Jesse, but they just call me Jessup," he said. "Ride along here for a bit toward the chuck box, and I'll be back." And with that, he rode toward the nearest rider, and they spoke for less than a minute.

Jessup returned, but the other rider dropped back and cut across through the center of the string of cattle and made his way to the chuck wagon while we took the long way around behind the herd. He spoke as he reined in next to me. "Gabe said we was gonna set 'em to millin' at the head of this little valley anyhow, so he's gonna get Sanders to stop and set camp on the rise yonder. With the wind from the north, it should keep the flies pushed away from night grub. Gabe says he'd be glad for the comp'ny 'round the fire."

"Is Gabe the trail boss?" I asked as we turned east toward the rear of the herd.

"No. Not so's you'd notice," he replied but didn't offer any more, so I didn't ask.

We rode around the herd to the north side, and even though we were some distance from the cows, I could feel the heat from their bodies between the gusts of wind.

We talked about the trail conditions and the weather and slowly gaining on the wagon when I pulled the roan to a stop. The chestnut that Jessup was riding only made two more steps before he was stopped as well. I noticed that he had also spun his horse so that when he stopped, his gun hand was away from me. I also noticed that his hand was already on his gun.

Jessup looked back at me and asked, "What is it?"

I pointed and said, "That black calf there. Is there something wrong with it?" I was looking at what looked like an ugly, seemingly disfigured, curly-haired calf.

Jessup relaxed his hold on his pistol. "You ain't been around trail herds a'fore, have you?" He shook his head in mock disgust and said, "That there is a buff. A buff'lo, I mean. They get caught up in near ever' herd cross these here parts. Why, there's pro'lly eight, mebee ten, in the herd right now. Couple buff'lo cows too. Sometimes, when you run across a herd of buffs, you gain a few head, but mostly you just lose cows." He started on again and continued, "Ever get a bull in there, you'd best kill 'im right out. Won't be nothin' but trouble, and they don't herd worth a sawed-off, ten-cent piece."

Still looking back at the young calf, I followed him up to where the wagon had stopped. I heard him say as he rode up, "Sandy, This here's Ty. He'll be breakin' bread with us tonight, so keep the buff chips out of the soup."

Sandy stood from unhitching his team of horses stretching his lower back and eyed me curiously.

"Glad to know ya," he said with a grin. Then he looked back at Jessup and asked, "Are ya goin' soft there, old man? This is the first one in two weeks that you've brought to the fire without a bullet hole in him." His grin widened as he looked back at me.

Jessup replied matter-of-factly, "He aint tried to cut the herd yet, has he?" And with that, he dismounted and started helping Sandy unhook the traces and the harnesses from the wagon team.

When they were loose, Sandy waved his hands toward them and shooed them out of camp. Another rider swung in and hazed them out toward the remuda. A young boy of around sixteen rode in with an armload of wood and dropped it close to a wagon wheel. When I turned my head and looked out at the cattle, there were two men already turning the lead cows back into the herd, causing the whole mass to spread out and start milling about.

I got the impression of a routine that had been practiced many times in the past, and everyone seemed to have a job and knows just what to do without much in the way of conversation.

It took less than thirty minutes to completely set up the camp and have a large pot hung over a hot fire with the smell of beans and wood smoke drifting in the wind. Sandy was standing at the rear of the wagon kneading some bread dough, and Jessup had just sat on a wooden box next to him and already had a cup of coffee in his hands.

A small, wiry man with a long graying beard and small black eyes rode up to the fire and spoke directly to Sandy. "Next clean water is a crick fifteen, mebee, sixteen mile west. Ain't been 'nuff rain fer Hodges crick ta be mor'n juss mud. Less'n we was ta swing to tha south 'bout ten mile to tha lake."

I caught the movement as Sandy's eyes quickly darted to Jessup and then back to the speaker. "Any tracks?" Sandy asked as he kind of shifted his feet nervously. "I mean, anyone on the trail ahead?"

Jessup stood and said, "I think it's all right, Cooper. I don't think Ty here is a part of that outfit from Missouri." He looked at me and continued, "No offense to ya, Ty, but I think even a cow thief would know the diff'ernce 'tween a buff an a longhorn calf."

He turned back to Cooper and asked, "Did you see anything out there that would keep us from reaching that creek tomorrow?"

Cooper shook his head. "Not if'n we get a early start an' keep movin'. They's good grass most of tha way. 'Bout six mile out we'll hafta cross a stretch what got burned mebee a week past but it ain't too wide. Couple o' hills yonder too, but they ain't yokers."

"Good," Jessup said. "When the herd gets settled, send in everybody but Gabe, and you two stay with the herd 'til we eat. Then I'll send Otto and Simmons to spell you."

Cooper rode off, and I stepped down from the saddle and tied the roan to the front of the wagon. I walked back toward Sandy, and Jessup said, "Sorry, Ty. Again, no offense to ya. I'm the segundo for this drive, and the boys are just lookin' out for me. That Missouri bunch has been known to ride in, find out who's in charge, and shoot the trail boss and then run the herd off in the confusion before someone steps up and starts makin' decisions."

I smiled. "None taken." I stopped next to the fire and asked, "So that's what all the talk about the two guns was for?"

"Yep," he replied, "I ain't never seen you before, and I ain't about to take any chances with another man's herd."

"I don't blame you there," I said. "Hey, what was it that Cooper said about the hill? A yoker I think he said."

Sandy laughed. "Ha, you must be from aways over yonder. A *yoker* is a hill that is too steep for the chuck wagon and a single team, and the horses have to be helped up to the top. With a yoke and another team."

Jessup said, "Ease up there, Sandy. Not everyone was born so far south that they had to make up their own words like us." He turned to me and said, "Soon's the biscuits are done, you'd better dish up a plate. The hands will be stampeding in here in about ten minutes, and if your hand's too close to the pot, you're liable to get it bit off."

Off in the distance, I could hear someone singing something about his Knoxville girl and how she was floating through Knoxville town. It was a ways off, and I couldn't tell for sure.

Jessup introduce me around the fire. He pointed out Otto, Frank, Simmons, and the teen named Skit. "You already met Cooper, and Gabe will be in after a bit," he explained.

We ate biscuits and beans with some kind of meat bobbing around in the pot. It was actually pretty good since I hadn't had beans in a while. What I really wanted was a can of peaches.

When I thought of that, a chill ran down my back, and I got a few odd looks from Skit and Otto when I shuddered.

The hands talked about the things they had seen in the course of the day: a red cow with a cut on the front leg, a brindle with on open sore, a limping calf, and numerous other bits of day-to-day observations.

Jessup looked up at Otto and said, "Ot, you and Simmons take first watch. I'll have Frank and Skit spell you at midnight."

Neither man spoke. They just got up and rode to the remuda where they roped fresh horses and moved their saddles to the new mounts.

"Ty," Jessup said as he put his plate on the wagon gate, "you feel up to riding with me to that tree line yonder to look for some fresh meat?"

"Sure," I said, finishing my coffee. I dropped my plate and cup at the wagon and presented my approvals to the cook. I the untied the roan and climbed on board.

"Let's get us some fresh horses first," he said as we moved away from the wagon.

I patted the roan on the neck and replied, "Thanks, but I'll stick with this one. He and I sort of know each other."

"Suit yourself," he said.

I followed Jessup to the remuda where he shook out a loop and dropped it over the head of a little, mouse-colored gelding about fourteen hands tall. He led the fresh pony away from the other horses toward me then dismounted. Both horses stood still as he switched the saddle and bridle from one to the other.

He remounted and rode toward the horses again where he roped a sorrel mare and fastened a lead rope on her. Riding to where I sat, he handed me the lead rope and then said, "Let's go. I spotted some antelope over here earlier, but I'm hoping for a deer or an elk myself. I like it better than antelope."

"Never had it myself," I said. "Antelope, I mean."

The sun was falling toward the horizon and it would be gone in another hour, so we didn't have much time. We talked as we rode and I told my story of the Lanauxe's.

He listened and occasionally asked a question or made a comment.

After I had my story out, he began to tell me about the herd cutters that they had run into along the trail. "The last raid," he said, "I'm almost sure was white men dressed to look like Indians."

"Why would anyone go to that much trouble away out here?" I asked.

"I can only figure that they plan on raiding herds and wagon trains and trying to put the blame off on the Indians so that no one will suspect them," he said as we continued to ride. "Then they can sell the stolen goods and stock to mining camps or back east to a trading post."

We stopped on a small rise where we could see the trees two hundred yards off, and immediately, we saw three deer. It looked like a doe and two yearling fawns right up next to the trees.

"Do you want me to hold the packhorse while you ride closer to get a shot?" I asked.

He eyed me quizzically and said, "These three horses is the only reason we might even get a shot. Check your load and keep that old smoke pole across your saddle."

As he slowly moved his horse closer to the trees at an angle and not directly at the deer, he explained, "You see, a lone animal moving right at 'em would most likely spook 'em. This way, we have three animals, two with tall lumps on 'em and one with no lump, moving sort of closer but not right at 'em. They'll watch, but they won't run long as we move slow like. Then after the shooting stops, we'll have meat."

"Oh, I understand," I said. "Kind of fooling them with a disguise."

"Yep," he said, "works most every time with the wild game that ain't used to folks."

He paused at the lower end of the slope that stretched up to where the deer still stood with their heads up. "It's about seventy yards from here. How's your shooting eye?" he whispered.

"Fair, I suppose." I said and slowly raised my Hawken rifle.

"Just take the small one on the right," he said. "That'll keep us in meat for a couple days and the other one will still have a momma."

The shot echoed briefly across the low hills, and two of the deer disappeared into the trees instantly. The third seemed to stagger in confusion for about two seconds, and then he fell in his tracks.

As the echo died away, Jessup was already moving toward the downed animal, and in less than five minutes, we had dressed the kill and tied it in place on one of the spare horses. I took the time to reload before dismounting just to be on the safe side.

"Will your men come to investigate the shot?" I asked as we turned to ride back

He responded with a chuckle. "No. They won't come." He paused to look around then continued, "If we was in trouble, there would be more than one shot. If someone shot at us first, then there would be no reason to come running 'cuz we'd be dead. The business we are in, you got to think of the herd first, and they can't be left unguarded."

When we got back, he told the story of my great hunting skills and how he got us so close that I could have touched the deer with the rifle before I fired. We all shared a few good-natured chuckles before we rolled up in our blankets and slept.

Shortly after midnight, I was awakened by the sound of low murmuring and talking at the fire as two men sat and sipped steaming coffee. They finally rose and walked to their horses, and not long after, I heard boots sliding through the grass as the night riders came in and found their beds for the night.

I lay awake in my blankets for a while listening to the distant click of horns and occasional lowing of a cow or two. Slowly, my eyes closed, and I finally drifted into a fitful sleep.

Before daybreak, Sandy was up stoking the fire and slicing bacon into a large skillet. The bacon was served with beans and more biscuits and hot black coffee and very little talk among the men. Then, as if on a silent command, the camp emptied, and the herd started moving again.

Sandy was packing the last of his cooking utensils and offered the last round of coffee before the fire was put out, when I said my thanks and followed Jessup out to the front of the herd. I rode along with him and watched as he hazed in a few energetic cows that wanted to run the other way. "Bunch quitters," one man call them. We talked about cows, horses, trails, and such as we moved along.

When we came to the stretch of grass that had been burned off by a wildfire, that's where I decided to leave the herd and head north again. I thanked Jessup and warned him again of those that followed me. He assured me that if they wanted to talk to him, they'd have to ride hard because he wasn't about to stop. I waved my so longs to those that were close by and headed out on my own again.

I had never seen a smoother-run organization in all my born days, and I even said so before I left.

My thoughts of the past turned into worries of tomorrow here in the cabin as I rolled over in my bunk and contemplated my half-finished bow and, of course, the wolf. Somewhere along there, I slept.

11

The next morning, I took my time before going out. I sat at the table and worked on my bow. I had decided to skip breakfast for a couple of reasons. The most obvious reason was that I had no food. And sometimes, I try to keep for spoiling myself with things like a full belly and such. Slows a man down.

I waited until the sun was well above the trees, and a warm wind had started to melt the snowdrifts and the ice hanging from the eaves. I had heard one time that this was called a *chinook* or "warming wind." They have been known to change the temperature in an area by twenty or thirty degrees in just an hour or two. But I knew that winter wasn't over yet. There could be a storm tomorrow that might dump three feet of snow in a few hours.

By then, I had the bow almost down to its final shape, and as soon as I had my bowstring made, I could begin testing the limbs to make sure they pulled evenly.

I put away the bow and cleaned the pile of shavings from the floor and stood up. It was slow mornings like this one that made me long for the rich smell of coffee on the stove.

I put on my coat, but I knew, by the look and smell of the weather, I would probably end up with it tied behind the saddle before the day was over. I wasn't fooled, though. That old Mother Nature is a devious sort. She was just giving me a chance to let my guard down before she moved back in.

I went out on the porch with a quick survey of the surrounding tree line then made my way to the barn.

The roan was in better spirits when I led him out of the stall and strapped the saddle in place, and to my relief, he didn't complain when I pulled the cinch tight. I mounted, and we walked through the trees to the original water hole I had cut in the ice. I dismounted, and as I removed the ax from the saddle, the wolf came out of the trees and sat down less than twenty feet from me. The roan shied nervously, but the wolf just looked at both of us with her ears up and tongue wagging. Since I knew the horse was unsure of the situation, I held the reins in one hand as I walked to the hole and removed the thin covering of ice that sealed the water below. I led the roan to drink, but he shuffled around the hole until he could keep the wolf in view before he dipped his muzzle in the cold water.

Seeming to sense the roan's nervousness, the wolf rose to her feet and padded back about fifteen feet back toward the tree line and sat back down in the snow. Watching us with only partial attention, she kept looking back north into the trees. I kept an eye on her while we drank, hoping she would spot any game moving through the trees and give me time to react.

When the roan was no longer inclined to drink, I moved him back to the trail to give the wolf access to the hole. I fussed with the bridle and latigo for a minute while I kept my eyes busy in the trees looking for movement. I seemed to have that odd feeling again of someone or something out there. Maybe I was getting jumpy and reading too much into the actions of a nearly starved-out wolf and an old, raw-boned nag of a horse. Of course, I didn't say that out loud so's a certain someone wouldn't get mad at me again.

I finally mounted and started moving toward the line of snares to see if I would eat that day or simply have to tighten my belt again. As we moved into the trees, I watched the wolf fall into pace about forty yards to the right, and she seemed content to follow and watch as we checked our traps. We had gone no more than fifty yards when I could see that we had a problem.

I could see the first snare through the trees ahead, and the snow around its location was trampled and discolored with the blood of what should have been my breakfast.

I rode forward and read the story in the snow. By the look of the tufts of fur left strewn about, I had caught a marten. Or maybe a mink. It was hard to tell with such small pieces left in evidence.

The animal had been caught tightly in the drag snare and was most likely struggling for its freedom when it was attacked. According to the sign left on the ground, the lynx had jumped from a nearby log and killed the helpless catch. Normally, a lynx, or any cat for that matter, will take the kill to a safer location to consume it, but here, the prey was tied to a bush. So the next best thing was to eat it there… and fast.

I was disappointed, of course, but couldn't actually bring myself to be mad. After all, the lynx was surviving on whatever he could find just like me. I was thinking—no—actually, I was hoping and praying that maybe he would have satisfied his appetite for the time being and I would get the next meal. But that was not to be the case.

The area around the next drag snare told almost the same story word for word; only it was a rabbit that was the main dish this time. A few bits of hair, blood, and numerous tracks were all that remained here too.

My disappointment was rapidly growing into irritation, and I knew that if something didn't change, my belly would be some upset later too. I said as much to the roan, but he reminded me that there was plenty of hay in the barn and that he would be most happy to share it with me.

I'm glad he couldn't see the expression on my face at the offer. He might have been grinning at the thought of me eating hay with him, but I'm sure he was truly sincere.

Maybe I could use the hay to fatten him up and...right then I was some disgusted with myself. The roan had carried me all these miles with no more than a few complaints, and I owed him something for that. And he'd probably be tougher than an old weather-worn boot to know the truth.

The roan stopped suddenly with his head up and ears pointed. I was sure for a minute that he had read my thoughts, but his attention was on the trees to the right. When I looked around, I could see that the wolf had disappeared too.

After we waited for about five minutes, I decided that there was nothing there to be seen and urged the roan forward toward the deadfall trap that marked my last hope for a meal for this morning.

As I approached the deadfall trap, I could see that the log was down. I was hoping that maybe with the log on top of the animal, the lynx wouldn't have been able to get to it. But when I swung the roan around the last tree, I was shocked to see the lynx was actually digging under the log. I had to stop him or I was going to go hungry. I jumped off the horse and grabbed the ax and raised it high overhead for a blow when I suddenly realized that the lynx had stopped moving.

He was dead.

Then it all made sense. The lynx had been just ahead of me on the snare line eating each catch then running off to the next one. His mistake was that he assumed this was a snare as well with the porcupine in it. When he jumped in and grabbed the raw pelt, he was struck on the back by the log and was merely in his death throes and convulsions when I arrived.

Lowered the ax and tried to hide my embarrassment from the Roan. I knew he was still grinning from his earlier remarks, and I didn't want him to have something else to gloat about.

I set the ax against the base of a tree and bent forward to check the cat. I wasn't going to lift the log until I was sure that there was no chance that it was still alive. Not only did I want to make sure that the thief was really dead but also that my meal wouldn't run away.

Yes. I was going to eat a cat. I don't claim any self-righteousness, and I ain't never been sanctimonious about anything as far as food goes. The bald fact was that I was that hungry.

After I shook his hind leg and prodded his side a few times, I lifted the log with my shoulder and dragged the still-warm body out of the trap. Tossing the cat to the side, I grabbed the short limb I had used before and wedged it under the log between the upright trees. I checked the bait, and it was frozen but otherwise unchanged from the day before.

The log had broken one of the notched sticks, and I was about to turn and look for a suitable replacement when the roan got my attention with a deep neigh and a stamped foot in the snow. I quickly looked at him and followed his gaze to the trees to his right. There was an Indian sitting on his horse not thirty yards away watching us.

My reaction was swift and sure. I dropped to a crouch and reached back with my right hand and drew my pistol and leveled it for a shot. I quickly realized that I must have dropped the gun in the snow. Then my mind registered that my hand had never found my pistol. Then the cold wave of reality hit me and I remembered that I was defenseless.

I stood and dropped my hands to my sides and waited. The Indian was a man of medium build with a tanned buckskin shirt and breeches. He had another darker skin tied around his shoulders, and he wore knee-high moccasins laced tightly around his legs. His long, black hair was spilling down over his back and was adorned with three feathers that drifted lazily in the slight breeze. His face was covered by brown leathery skin and seamed with lines and creases of age. In his left hand, he held a beautifully made bow, and a quiver full of arrows hung across his back.

I guessed his age to be about sixty, but I could tell from his stature and appearance that he would be a tough man to fight in a scuffle. And he had me dead to rights even though he didn't have an arrow nocked.

We stood like that for some time, and I continued to run possibilities through my head to seek the best advantage I could find. I had the ax against the tree a few feet behind me, but I would have to wait until he got close enough before I could use it. It would do me no good to run even if I could make it to my horse because I had nowhere to go. He would have an arrow headed straight at me as soon as I made the first move toward the ax or my horse anyway.

I had resigned myself to the fact that I had no other option but to stand there, and I think the Indian realized that. When my shoulders dropped in quiet acceptance of the situation, he finally spoke, but it was in a language I wasn't familiar with.

When I didn't respond, he spoke again and gestured with his bow. I took it, by the sound of his words and indicating motions, that the wanted me to mount and ride ahead of him. I pointed at the dead cat, and he made a scooping motion with his hand, so I bent and lifted the carcass by the back feet.

I took a step toward the roan, and then I changed direction and picked up the ax slowly. I carried it to the roan and tied it securely behind the saddle. With a rawhide string, I tied the cat's four paws together and hooked them over the horn and then climbed aboard the roan.

When I looked toward the old warrior, he simply pointed west, so I pulled the reins around until we were pointed west and urged the roan into a walk.

I had no idea where we were going, but our horses walked for an hour. We crossed the ice-covered stream in the first half mile and the negotiated several hills and gullies. He grunted and pointed a new path or direction from time to time, but we kept moving generally west.

Eventually, we topped out on a small rise overlooking a shallow valley with five tepees nestled in the lee of the trees. There were three fires burning in the circle of the lodges and several women moving around the camp. There were eleven horses standing close by, and I could see that they were hobbled to limit their movements.

When we started down the hill, one of the women spoke sharply, and they all turned to look in our direction. Six children of various ages came out of the largest lodge to the center of camp and stopped to watch our approach. There were subdued murmurs in the crowd as we rode through the center of the lodges, and as I looked them over, I noticed that there were no grown men anywhere to be seen.

The old warrior rode forward and, by placing the end of the bow on the roan's nose, stopped my horse in front of the oldest lodge by the look of the hides. He used the bow to point at me then at the ground, indicating that I was to dismount. So I did.

At least, he didn't bother to tie my hands, and if the chance to run did present itself, I vowed to be ready.

He spoke to one of the older women, and after a brief reply, she stepped forward and removed the lynx from my saddle and walked away with it. He pointed at another woman and spoke in a softer, more even tone, and she turned and disappeared into the lodge without a word.

Two of the oldest children stepped forward when the warrior dropped to the ground, and his pony and the roan were led away. He stopped in front of me and began to speak in a louder tone. As he talked, I got the idea that he wasn't speaking to me. He was telling the others something about me while we stood face to face. With end of the bow, as he continued, he pointed at my boots then at the empty holster at my side then at my chest. He walked around behind me and continued speaking. I felt the bow tip slide under my left wrist, and he lifted it for all to see my bruised and swollen left hand.

After he finished, two of the remaining women stepped forward and each took an arm, and they led me into the lodge where the first woman had disappeared earlier. When we entered, all I could see in the dark was a small fire ring of stones with a few smoldering coals burning in the center and another, older woman beyond the fire. I was guided around the fire and, with hand motions, indicated to sit.

At least, that's the way I took it. With a slender finger pointed at the ground and a single word spoken as a command accompanied by two hands on my shoulders pushing me down, I sat. One woman built up the fire and placed several fist-sized rocks on the edge of the coals. Then all three of them turned and left me there alone.

When my eyes had adjusted to the dim light after a few minutes, I began to survey my surroundings. There were stacks of raw, dried furs and bundles of cured hides to my right. Several baskets were stacked on my left, and by the look and smell, I could tell that these were full of dried meat and grain. Behind me, there was a hide rolled into a long bundle about four feet long and tied with several leather strings.

I continued to study my surroundings and tried to remember all I had been told of Indians from other travelers and those who had encountered them before.

It was about an hour later and I was running out of things to contemplate when two of the women from earlier came back in with a large clay pot. They set the pot near the coals, and both busied themselves with their own tasks. I asked them their names, and they didn't even acknowledge that I had spoken.

One woman busied herself by looking over my left hand. She pushed here and prodded there, but I wasn't about to give her any indication that I hurt even though she kept looking up to see if I would react. The other woman looked to me like she was preparing a meal, but with her back to me I couldn't see for sure. She kept grinding things on a flat rock and adding them to her mixture. She finally added some water and stirred it all together and placed it by the fire.

The rocks in the fire were hot and charred, and the first woman, with a forked stick in each hand, expertly lifted the smoking rocks and dropped them into the pot of water. It didn't take long for the whole pot of water to start steaming.

The second woman continued to stir her smaller pot with the aromatic mixture in it.

After a minute or two, to my surprise, they both stood and grabbed me by the arms and forced me to my feet. They began removing my coat, my hat, and both shirts until I was stripped to the waist. They each took a piece of cloth and, after dipping it in the hot water, began to wash me from head to waist. Every swipe of the damp cloth seemed to find a bruise or cut from my tumble down the mountain. I was too scared to move, but all that warm water just about fairly got me relaxed and sleepy except when they hit a sore spot. I was made to hold my arms straight so they could get at the underside of each and to my ribs.

The woman on the left stopped washing when she got down to my wrist. I was then dried off and forced to sit back down on the same spot.

I wasn't sure what to think, and I've never heard of anyone washing a prisoner then dragging them out to their death, but like I said before, I don't know much about their Indian ways.

I was almost relaxed to the point of not caring if they were planning on killing me after this or not.

My left hand was placed in a small pot filled with the warm water and left there while they both took handfuls of the mixture in the other pot and began to smear it across my back and shoulders and down my chest. I got the idea that it was some kind of medicinal poultice when I became aware that they were both repeating a rhythmic chant as they worked. It sort of reminded me of how I had seen Ma put a layer of herbs and spices on a large roast one time.

The one on the right stopped and handed me a gourd dipper half full of a milky brown substance and indicated that I should drink it. When the hot, bitter liquid touched my tongue, I almost choked, but she was persistent and made me drink it all. The other one pulled my hand out of the warm water and began to rub it with the same concoction they had put on my back. When she got to the little finger, I winced at the pain, but she applied gentle, steady pressure, and I was able to endure.

I noticed that my thoughts were coming in halting staggers, and all the pain in my body, including my hand, was becoming a distant memory. I fell back onto the pile of skins and closed my eyes. I didn't move for a long time, and my head swam with confusion each time I tried to look around. I was enveloped by a sense of well-being, and my mind drifted into the darkness within, and I slept.

When I awoke later, it was full of light outside and maybe getting on toward evening, so I must have slept through the night and all day. I sat up with a swimming head and realized that the poultice had been washed away and now I had my shirt back on. It had been cleaned and mended.

My mind was still muddling through and trying to register my surroundings when I smelled food and realized that I was near to starving and my throat was dry. I was handed a gourd dipper, and after sniffing and tasting the liquid, I was relieved to know that it was simply water. I emptied it in four long gulps and reached for more, but the dipper was taken from me, and a bowl of soup was placed in my hands. As I ate, I could taste the meat and some sort of root cooked into the brew, and when it was gone, my stomach screamed for more. I was offered the dipper again, but I pushed it aside and shook the bowl indicating I wanted more soup and was rewarded with a full bowl and several laughs and snickers.

That's when I realized that the large room was full of people. Or at least appeared to be.

As I looked around in the dim light, I counted fourteen in attendance, but, including the old warrior on my right, there were still only four adult men.

I emptied the second bowl of soup and another gourd full of cold water and then looked quietly at the crowd. I figured that if they were going to kill me, it wouldn't be today because I was going to live long enough to eat some more of that soup, and I would probably have to apologize to Miss Ellie sometime later, but right now she was a close second where cooking was concerned.

The old man that brought me in grunted and pointed to my left hand. When I looked down, I could see that it was wrapped tight in a soft, thin hide. It was wrapped almost like a glove, and it left all my fingers exposed for use, and I realized that there was no swelling and no pain. I could still see some of the bruising along each finger, but when I flexed my hand, it didn't hurt. It was still weak and stiff and I was sure I had little gripping strength, but I wasn't going to complain.

When I look back to the old man, he was smiling. Everyone here was smiling, which made me grin like an idiot. We passed a long, decorated pipe back and forth a couple of times, and while we smoked there wasn't one word spoken. It was almost an eerie silence, but I understood it to be some sort of ceremony, so I just followed and did likewise. When the pipe was placed to the side, the talking livened up, and an old woman stepped forward holding a turtle shell in her hand. There was a scented smoke rising from the bowl, and she went around us twice with a fan made of feathers softly blowing the smoke over and around our heads. She was chanting much like the women when they applied their poultice mixture.

There was much talk among the tribe, but I could catch nary a word. I knew I was the subject of the discussion, but I found no way to contribute or contradict, so I sat quiet. It wasn't long before the old warrior stood and raised his hands for silence. He spoke for a minute and made some left-handed and then some right-handed gestures then he pointed at me and said something in a loud voice, and it seemed that everyone in the lodge smiled with excitement.

I had not the first idea of what just happened, but they stood me up and began clapping me on the back and dancing around me. I looked at the old man, and he just stood there smiling.

Later, after everyone had gone, the old man sat by the fire, staring into the dying coals. He spoke quietly from time to time, and with his hand gestures, I sort of got the idea that he wanted something from me, but I had no idea what it could be.

After a while, he just laid back and pulled a skin around him and went to sleep. I sat for a while looking around and contemplating, but I finally did the same, and my dreams were filled with memories of my travels after leaving the cattle herd.

12

With the cattle herd three days behind me, I had been longing for conversation again. I was mostly an old lobo and didn't mind being by myself for long stretches, but the one thing that was hard to get used to when you leave folks is the lack of conversation. Maybe it's getting used to not having the back and forth with a different point of view. I suppose that's why most cowboys and mountain men talk to their horses or even themselves. Here lately, though, I seemed to be doing a lot of forth without much back from the Roan.

It occurred to me that maybe we were both just tired of all the travel and needed a break. I hadn't seen or heard any pursuit on my back trail for some time, so I decided to start looking for a place to hole up for a while.

I came across this little creek around midafternoon, and I decided to stop for the day. Sort of rest up and give the roan a chance to see if he could digest this prairie weed that was growing around here.

The little draw that hid the creek was only about ten feet deep and had only one or two small trees close by. Knowing from experience that prairie storm miles away can catch a man unaware with all the runoff water, I decided to travel downstream and locate a more suitable location. I descended into the draw and began to follow the meandering stream when I noticed several sets of unshod horse tracks.

Since the trails were not drifting from grass to shrub to water and the like, I was certain that they weren't part of a wild band but being ridden by men, most likely Indians, and there looked to be only four of them. And that's when I saw something that fairly sent shivers down my back like a bucket of cold rainwater.

There were barefooted tracks of a girl or a small boy in the mud next to the stream. The hoof tracks were on top of some of the footprints, so the Indians were following or chasing the runner. The tracks were fairly fresh, so I removed the thong that held my pistol in place and checked the charge in my Hawken then urged the roan forward. My better judgment told me to hook the roan's nose to the North Star and spur him out of the country, but when have I ever done the sensible thing?

After about a quarter mile, the draw was getting deeper, and the sides were growing steeper. The stream lazily drifted from one side to the other, so I had to cross it several times, but it was only two feet wide.

The last time I crossed, I could see where one of the Indian ponies had stepped in the edge of the water, and there was still muddy water swirling next to it. That told me they had been here within the last few minutes. I looked as far down the draw as I could see, but there was still no movement . I rode forward until I came to a sharp right-hand bend in the draw that had now become at least thirty feet across. I rode to the far-right bank just before the curve and stopped the roan in the shadows of a large sycamore tree growing on the upper bank and listened.

I heard the loud crack of a slap, like the sound of a hand on exposed flesh and the sound of a girl scream in pain. With my rifle held against my shoulder, I eased my horse forward until I had four men and a young Indian girl in view.

The first shock was that they were speaking English and some Spanish. The second shock was that they weren't Indians. They were riding Indian ponies, but they were most certainly not Indians. I suddenly realized that these were the men that Jessup had spoke of, or at least some of them. There were four here, but where were the others? Jessup told me there was a dozen or more. If they were close and I got into a fight, then I'd be in trouble, but that was of little worry right at that moment.

Two of them were still on their horses, and the other two were on the ground looking down at a young Indian girl sobbing with her head buried in her hands.

They were only forty yards off, but they were having so much fun laughing and cursing that they never heard me until I spoke.

"I wouldn't do that again," I said as I sighted on the two men with the girl.

I spoke loud, but the one next to the girl already had his hand wrapped around a three-foot club and had it raised high above his head. When the downward swing started, I shot him right through the brisket. The other one standing on the ground dove to his left behind a bush. As he made his move to dive, I put a bullet through his foot with my pistol just as he leaped off his feet.

The two mounted men spurred their horses toward the trees on the right, and I levered the hammer on the Colt and spun another load into position and sent a bullet in their direction, but I must have missed.

I jumped to the ground and kept my pistol pointed at the brush as I ran toward the girl. She looked up and screamed again as she saw me running at her. One of the men must have misjudged my location because he stood up behind a tree with his pistol drawn and looked back toward the roan. When I skidded to a halt and went down on my right knee, the movement must have caught his attention. Before he could determine if I was friend or foe, I had my pistol pointing at him.

When his eyes grew large with realization, he automatically raised his gun, and that was to be the last move he made. I shot him right through the throat where his two collarbones met.

Two down, one injured, and one still unscathed. I reached down to help the girl to her feet, and she slapped my hand away. She was still wide-eyed with terror, and I knew that my next best move was to draw fire away from her, so I ran to the left toward the brush. There had been no return fire up to this point, and I could see no movement, so I waited for about half a minute then stood up and advanced quickly to the spot where I had shot the last man. I found nothing but the dead man.

I heard a rustle of movement behind me, but as I spun, I only saw the girl running down the draw once more. I let her go.

I walked into the trees with the attention of a cornered lion, but all was quiet. After another minute, I heard the sound of hoofbeats retreating in the distance. I walked back to where the girl had been and found the man I had shot in the foot. He was dead.

He must have miscalculated his dive when the bullet tore through his foot because when he dove, his head smacked into a large rock. There was an indention in the top of this head, and he wasn't breathing.

I reloaded the pistol as I walked back to the roan and listened to the unnatural stillness left in the wake of deadly gunfire. I reloaded my rifle then mounted and walked my horse forward to see if I could locate the girl.

Her tracks were plainly visible in the mud and sand of the draw for the first fifty yards, but then she ran across a rock shelf and probably climbed out onto the higher plains. I backtracked a couple of times, but I never could find her sign again.

I wondered to myself how and why that lone girl was way out in the middle of this desolate country all alone.

With nothing further to be done for the girl, I turned back to the dead men. I would have checked their pockets, but they were in buckskins and moccasins, and they had no saddlebags either. One man had a pouch slung around his neck by a leather string, but all it contained was tobacco and a few shreds of paper to roll it in.

It was just like Jessup had thought. These men must have been a part of the ones trying to steal his herd and robbing the wagon trains along the trail. With the toe of my boot, I turned over the first man I had shot.

Well, there was three here that wouldn't ever be holding up any wagons again.

I figured that the right thing to do now was bury these men, but I wasn't going to take a chance of the Indians returning when that girl told them what happened. Other than my not being dressed like an Indian, there would be no way for them to tell that I wasn't one of the attackers.

When I mounted the roan again, he wasn't shy about letting me know that he was some unhappy with me. Maybe it was the fact that he was left out of the fight or maybe because I didn't tell him the plan of action before I went forward so he could do his part.

I tend to think that he was just being over protective, and he thought I was going to get my fool head shot off. I smiled. It kind of warmed me up on the inside to know I had someone worrying about me.

We headed north out of the draw after watering up. It seemed the best idea to give up on this resting spot, so tired or not, we went.

13

I was pulled back to the present when the old Indian, sleeping across the fire from me, moaned and grunted in his sleep.

I rolled over and pulled the skins tighter around my shoulders and drifted off to sleep with plenty of doubts and questions on my mind.

When I awoke in the lodge the next morning, I was surprised that I was alone. I would have bet that no man could get up and walk out of a room without me knowing it, sleeping or not. That brown liquid must still have some kind of hold on me. Or at least that's what I told myself.

When I donned my coat and went outside, it was nearly light enough to see, and I immediately saw that the old warrior was standing there next to the fire with the other three adult men I noticed the night before. When I approached the group, one of the women handed me a wooden bowl filled with boiled meat, and I set to with a purpose.

There was some kind of greens in the dish as well along with some nuts and something that must have contained the minerals I needed because it hit the spot. It didn't take long to finish and was some sad to see that they were already cleaning up and putting away.

I stood and took a long drink from the water skin that was hanging nearby and wiped my hand across my mouth.

The old warrior spoke in my direction and gestured for me to join him and the other three warriors standing near the last lodge. They each held a horse, and the one on the right had my roan as well as his own horse. He handed me the reins and indicated for me to mount. I wanted to check to saddle, for I'm not a very trusting man, but I figured I would wait so I didn't offend the one who saddled up for me. I took it to be the one who handed me the reins because he watched me with curiosity for a while after I mounted.

The old warrior spoke to the small crowd gathered nearby and then mounted on his pony then led us away from the village at a fast trot.

The rest of us sunk a heel in and followed along, and I still had no idea where they were taking me. So far, they hadn't shown any hostile intent and had treated me with nothing but kindness now that I think back on it.

I took a minute to look at each of my companions, and I decided that, aside from being older than most warriors that I had seen, these would be very tough and hard to handle in a scrap. Right then, I was glad that I was with them and not being chased by them.

We were heading west toward the far horizon over a bleak, flat, wintery landscape that still held deep snowdrifts on the ground, and the trees were still mostly covered with snow despite the warm winds of the past twenty-four hours. I could see for nearly two miles in the morning light. At the cabin, I had always been surrounded by forest on the eastern, southern, and western sides then mountains to the north. At the most, even down the frozen stream, the visibility was never more than one hundred yards. The Indians talked quietly among themselves as we rode, and I listened for any words that I might be familiar with, but after a while I decided that I would have to be content with the view.

After a time, with nothing better to do as we rode, I decided to give these men names to go by. The old one who brought me here I called Wise One because it seemed that when he spoke, most folks just listened. The one that saddled my horse was about 5'10" and 160 pounds, and I figured he would smash anything he ran over, so I called him Iron Horse like them newfangled steam engines. The one in the lead up there was over 6' and had to be pushing 200 pounds, and I'd bet if you boiled him dry, there wouldn't be an ounce of fat rendered. I called him Oak. The last man looked to be strong, reliable, and smart, but there was something about him that made me look again. He had the look of a man that could go plumb loco on you in the heat of a fracas, so I called him Powder Keg, but it didn't take long until it was shortened to just Keg.

Now I know these men couldn't understand a thing I was saying, but on the off chance that one of them knew a touch of English or found an interpreter, I decided to shoot straight with them when it came to talking time even though they gave no indications of understanding. Not to mention that if I made them mad, they were armed and I still had no guns, although they had made no moves to take my knife or the ax.

We rode the day through and traveled mostly to the west again and maybe about twenty miles south of where we started. We only stopped twice throughout the day to stretch and give the horses a breather, and I was beginning to admire the stamina of these men who rode the distance without a saddle.

Don't go to thinking that we were mistreating our stock in any way. The horses were allowed to take mouthfuls of any dried grass we found from time to time and whenever we crossed a stream or passed a water hole, we would punch through the thinning ice and allow them to drink.

We rode until it was nearing dark. There was only about an hour of light left, and the Wise One spoke to Iron Horse and pointed north, and then he turned to Keg and pointed south, and they both rode off in their appointed directions. Oak rode forward into a low fold in the hills, and when I started my horse forward, the Wise One held up a hand for me to stop. We sat there for a span of five minutes when we heard a horse returning back up the hill.

When Oak came into view in front of us, he motioned us forward with a wave of his hand, and we urged our mounts to follow. We dropped into a small copse of trees with a spring bubbling happily nearby. There was a fire burning in a well-used hollow of rocks, and I was curious how Oak had the time to start this fire and return so quickly. That's when I noticed that the fire had been burning for some time and there were thousands of tracks in the surrounding snow. There was a well-developed pile of coals and ashes, and if I had to guess, I'd say that the fire had been burning for several days.

When we pulled up and dismounted, Oak stepped over and took our horses and led them into the brush. The Wise One indicated that we would sit on a log that had been drug in close to the fire sometime in the past. There was a pile of wood close at hand, and from time to time, he would add a small stick or two, but for the most part we sat quietly. He occasionally spoke in low, conversational tones, but I had no answers for questions that I couldn't understand. I was nearly plumb over any notions that they meant to do me harm, but I still had no idea what their intentions were.

It was right about full dark when I heard footsteps coming through the trees, and Iron Horse stepped up to the fire with a haunch of venison and began slicing off chunks to be roasted over the fire. I could see that Keg and Oak were standing at the edge of the trees where we had entered, but I could also hear more movement behind us toward the spring.

Suddenly, the whole camp stood in startled shock as a lone wolf howled into the night from the top of the hill where we had sat our horses earlier. Except me, that is. I was as startled as all the Indians and maybe more so, but I had already been expecting the unexpected, so to speak.

There was an exclamation from behind us, and the sound of several feet shuffling in the snow and eight more Indians appeared in the firelight from behind us. There was excited talk and pointing among the group toward the source of the howl then back at me.

The Wise One was approached by another stately looking man of sixty or seventy years of age. They talked in low tones, and twice they had to quieten the talk of the others before they could continue.

The wolf howled again as if on cue, and another answered from the hills to the north. The sound wavered eerily in the night and died away into cold silence. I could see indecision and concerned looks forming on the faces of a few of the group, and I began to form an idea. I almost laughed out loud but managed to keep my wits about me and swallow the bubbles of laughter. I figured to make these folks wonder just who they had captured, so I stood and addressed the crowd.

I raised my hands to indicate that I needed quiet, but I started speaking before their protests died away. I said, "It appears that the presence of these wolves might have some of you a might worried." I paused for a brief instant to be sure I had everyone's attention then continued. "They mean you no harm, and they're probably just worried about where you might be taking me." I had a thought forming in my mind, and I had to weigh the good and bad of it first, but I decided to go ahead with it anyway. If this went bad, they might just kill me outright.

As I spoke, I looked each person in the eye for an instant. "I will tell my friends, the wolves, that you mean for no harm to come to me and that you are willing to be their friend as well as mine. I can't lie to them, so we must all be in agreement. Do you agree that you are our friend?" I continued to look at Wise One as I finished the question.

He nodded his head at the question and spoke a few words that sounded like a *yes* to me, although I doubt that he understood anything I said. So I laid into my plan. I nodded at him then turned toward the hill and leaned back, cupped my hands around the sides of my mouth, and howled like my life depended on it. And I think it sounded pretty good if you ask me.

To my relief, before my echoes had died away in the night, a wolf answered, and the howl was followed by a few excited yelps and several howls further in the distance. This brought a stunned reaction from the Indians that stood in front of us, and there was more excited talk passed back and forth.

Wise One looked at me with a sort of satisfied smile like he knew all along what I would do.

I thought about walking to the top of the hill, but I didn't want to push my luck and have the wolves run off into the night and everyone realize that I really had no communication with them after all.

The talk continued among the Indians for another hour in the darkness, and the wolves had fallen silent. Everyone began to eat, and things began to quiet down, and after a time, they began to leave in pairs and small groups to their own bedrolls. Oak appeared and beckoned me to a bedroll tucked back under a large spruce tree. I was beginning to feel like royalty and might have even enjoyed the feeling if I had some understanding of what the future held for me.

It was a quiet, uneventful night, and I slept surprisingly well. When crawled out from under the skins in the crisp predawn air, I stretched and yawned and flexed my hip to see if it would cause me any pain today. My hand was still wrapped in the soft hide, but I almost didn't have to favor it at all anymore. I folded the skins and moved to the fire and was some disappointed that I didn't see a coffeepot in the coals even though I hadn't had any for some time.

I paused by the fire next to Iron Horse and mumbled "Good morning" in his direction. He looked at me and smiled and pointed to a stack of corn cakes and dried meat strips lying on a skin next to the fire. Each small cake was about as big as my flat, opened hand and just over half an inch thick. I picked one up and bit into it and was surprised at the taste. It smelled like Ma's cornbread, but I could taste nuts and honey inside the cake. It was really good, and I only needed one, but I ate two anyway.

With the growing light of the new day, the camp slowly came to life, but with all the activity among the men, no one seemed to be packing up to leave. Each one seemed to busy themselves with normal camp tasks or just lying about as if waiting for something. I decided to relax and enjoy the day, and I surely didn't have to worry about any two-bit outlaws from New Orleans coming up on me here.

14

I judged the time to be near two or three in the afternoon when I noticed a slightly different buzz in the conversation of the camp. I stood from where I had been dozing against a tree listening to the music of the bubbling spring. There was some activity up on the hill where the wolf had been the night before, and I could see a small group of men walking toward us. There were six of the Indians from last night and one white man leading a pack mule.

At least that's what I think he was. He was as brown as any Indian, and he had long, dark hair falling from under his hat in wild tangles. He was covered in skins, and he carried a much-worn, well-oiled Kentucky-style flintlock rifle. His graying beard blew to the side in the cold breeze revealing a massive hairy chest visible between his open lapels. He wore black boots on his feet that came up to his knees. He walked straight at me until he was within ten feet of me, and he stopped abruptly.

He looked me over coolly for a full minute then spoke, "What be the name you use, boy?"

When I responded with "Ty Matthews," he turned to Wise One and spoke in what I assumed to be the Indian's tongue.

I knew there couldn't be a translation for my name, but I never did hear him say anything that sounded close to that in his talk with Wise One, but he did point at me several times.

After a few back-and-forth exchanges between them, the white man walked over and set down across the fire from Wise One and continued talking. After about thirty minutes, they both looked at me, and Wise One gestured for me to join them.

When I sat down, the white man said, "My name is Buffalo Tongue." Then he gestured toward the Indian and continued, "I was raised by Fast Elk here, and I spent thirty years of my livin' under his watchful eye. I've gone my way a huntin' gold yonder to tha high-up mountains. They fetched a runner out ta get me cuz you done stirred a ruckus with that there wolf business o' your'n."

I just looked at him with an awed expression, and he said, sternly, "Close yer mouth, boy. I know jus what ya got in yer noggin, an ya gotta get in yer skull that these Injuns ain't got tha same thinkin' as we'uns. They got it that yer some shakes cuz o' that wolf you been talkin' to."

"You mean they think those wolves are mine?" I asked with astonishment.

He replied in a calm and patient voice, "Listen here, Ty. Ya gotta quit actin' sa almighty shocked 'cuz these folks here believe in what their thinkin' 'bout you. If'n ya get 'em ta thinkin' it ain't so, they might'n just kill ya right out. Let's back up ta tha get-go, an' I'll give it to ya like they see it," he said with a wave of his hand.

"How long ya been in these parts? I mean afore ya met Running Elk here," he asked.

"In the area? Maybe two weeks, I suppose. I've been at the cabin less than a week," I replied.

He chuckled. "Well, 'parently, they been watchin' you mor'n, ya know. They got this wild tale 'bout how they been strugglin' ta keep meat in their lodges, an' many were sick an' in fear of dying when this last storm come in. Soons tha storm let up a mite, Fast Elk went t'ward tha peak yonder ta hunt an seek 'structions from tha Great Spirit. Tha's when he spied them wolf tracks. They set great store by tha wolf so he follered this'un. An' she was follerin' you." He leaned forward and stirred the fire and spoke to Wise One, or I guess now I should call him Running Elk.

After a few minutes, he turned back to me and continued his narrative. "Running Elk was wondern' why this 'ticular wolf was follerin' you like a pet. He's tellin' me that ever' other wolf in tha country is stalkin' man an' beast alike fer food. 'Cept this 'un, even when she was skin an' bone her own self, so he follered her sign. An' she follered yours. He tells me you rode a snow slide to tha bottom of a draw an' walked away."

He paused and looked at me, so I said, "That's true, but it was my own hardheaded stupidity that got me in that bind."

He chuckled again. "No matter tha reason. You got big medicine among 'em. He tol' me that you set some snares an' the wolf put her own self in tha trap. Mebee, he says, 'cuz she didn't know how to get up close to ya 'thout scarin' ya off. Or he thinks mebee tha wolf was offerin' herself to ya so's ya wouldn' starve."

My head came around sharply, and he held up a hand to quiet my exclamations. "I done tol' ya, mos' Injuns got differ'nt thinkin' than us. Don't mean it's wrong. Mebee we been tha one's that's got it wrong over all this time."

Running Elk spoke to him in low tones and many hand gestures, and then Buffalo Tongue turned back to me and said, "I was a young man o' thirty or there 'bouts when I ran inta Running Elk and his pa. They was yonder on tha plains an' Mayippa, Running Elk's pa, had just got tea kettled by an old buffler bull an' had a broke leg an' a dead horse. They was no way ta move 'im afore this ol' bull came back 'round.

"They done upped their bows an' shot 'im full o' arras, but he was still a snortin' an' pawin' fixin' ta charge. They was yet ta see a rifle like tha one I had and was plumb amazed when the gun barked, an' that ol' bull just laid down slick as ya please. I was some amazed my own sef 'cuz it ain't usual that a two-thousand-pound buff bull will lay down with jus one shot. I didn't know at tha time, but tha rest o' tha Injuns was watchin', an' from then on I was big medicine to these folks."

"Is that how you got the name Buffalo tongue?" I asked.

"Yep," he replied with a chuckle. "Funniest quirk ya did see too. That ol' bull was facin' us, and when I loosed that slug right at 'is neck, he bellered and dropped 'is head ta charge. That slug went in 'is mouth an' clean through 'is tongue an' jaw then struck 'im in tha heart. He was 'lmost dead anyhow from them arras an' I jus' blew out 'is wick."

"I can surely understand their thanks for that, but I didn't save anyone that I can remember," I said.

"That mebee tha way of it, but you bein' able to walk up and touch a wild wolf is mighty 'pressive ta a Injun. Running Elk seed ya his own self," he said.

I looked up in surprise and replied, "He was there? When the wolf...there was nobody around when I got the wolf out of the snare."

"Don't never underthink and Injun, Ty," he said with a grin. "Old Elk there said he had follered you ta see if'n you'd starve or not. And he seed ya walk up right to tha' wolf a'talkin' an jawin' tha whole time like you'uns was fam'ly. They set some pride by the wolf in these here parts, an' you done showed 'em that y' kin the wolf and their talk."

"I can't speak wolf, and you know it," I said, snorting.

He looked up with a serious expression on his face and said, "I don't know nothin' of tha' kind. And how would I? But what's most of importance, Running Elk believes it, and so does 'is people." He stirred the fire with a stick. "You might think that any man could'a walked up to a wolf an' pulled 'im outta that snare, but not so, my friend. Don't matter ta me one way or t'other, but it 'ppears that you don't believe in your own self." He stood and walked around the fire and sat beside me. "Ever one o' these Injuns heerd ya lass night when ya told that wolf that she didn't haf ta worry 'bout you and that you was in good hands with Running Elk and his people."

"How'd they get all that out of a couple of howls into the wind?" I asked.

With a smile he said, "'Cuz that's jus what I told them happened. I told them exact and to the letter what I thought fit the goin's on at tha time. An' ever since then, they been spottin' game ever trip. So they take that as strong medicine."

That evening, we traveled another two miles to the main Indian encampment of more than thirty lodges covered with buffalo, deer, and elk hides. There were a dozen cook fires and fifty or sixty people walking around the camp.

That night, there was a ceremony and a dance to celebrate their good fortune of their recent successful hunts. The dance, I was told, dated back to the ancient times and was passed down from their ancestors. And as if right on time during the performance, there was a lonely howl lifted toward the moon from a far-off hill several miles away. There were several excited exclamations and yells, and then the chants and singing resumed. It took me some time and a few comments from Buffalo Tongue to realize that they were celebrating because of me. Well, me and the wolf. They think we are the reason that the elk and deer have returned.

"They done give ya yer own Injun name," he said. "They call you Man Who Speaks with Wolf. I'm juss gonna call ya Wolf, but it means more than that. It means communication, or instruction, but it also means explanation and soothing tongue. Well, that's tha best meanin' I can give ya. You done been 'dopted in like a brother ta the whole tribe. You'd even be legal in their eyes if'n ya wanted ta take an Injun wife." He finished with a laugh.

I was worried at first. I didn't like the thought of them counting on me for something that I couldn't control. And I shuddered at the thought of a wife that I couldn't communicate with.

As the evening passed and my confidence grew then waivered time and again, I suddenly became aware that it wasn't me or the wolf that they were celebrating. It was the connection between man and animal that they valued. Me and the wolf simply represented that connection. Whether it was one of their own or an outsider like me didn't matter to them.

I laid my head down that night in a warm, comfortable lodge knowing that there was much more to our lives and existence than we will ever be able to imagine or understand.

I was up and out of the lodge with the first hints of light in the eastern sky. It had remained warm overnight or at least above freezing according to the steady drips of melting snow and ice hanging from nearby trees. There were few Indians up at this hour after such a festive evening, but I did spot an active cooking fire going, so I headed that way.

I could tell before I got close that the large, bulky figure seated by the fire was Buffalo Tongue. He sitting on the ground eating a chunk of deer meat he had roasted over the fire.

"Mornin', Talks to Wolf." He said with a smile.

"Mornin'," I said. "I guess I ain't Ty anymore." I smiled.

"Yep," he said, "you'll be whoever you are." He pointed away from camp and added, "Out there you'll be Ty, but when yer 'mongst these Injuns, you better be Speaks with Wolf." He laughed. "That was some hoorah las' night. These folk'll be makin stories 'bout you for a while." He looked at me curiously and said, "Ya could stay right here with 'em, ya know. They'd welcome you right in."

I waited a minute then replied, "I can't talk to them. I mean, I want to. This is the first time I've been in an Indian camp and I've got questions, but they wouldn't understand me."

"Same was fer me when I run up on Mayippa an' Running Elk. I couldn't speak their tongue, but seems like in no time I was palaverin' with 'em all day."

I looked at the fire thoughtfully and said, "I may come back, but I need some time first."

"Well," he said, "they're gonna be some sad ta see ya leave."

"I've got my own problems to handle. I need to get back to the cabin where I can be alone to think for a while."

"Mebee so." He grinned. "But you won't be alone for long." When I asked him why, he said, "Them trees and hills where that cabin is settin' in also jus' happens ta be tha best huntin' grounds 'round these parts in the early parts of tha year."

He stood and wiped his hands on his pants then looked at me with a serious expression. "I say again, you've been 'ccepted, Ty. All funnin' aside, you are a part of these Injuns now, whether you like it or no. An' they're gonna 'spect you ta look out fer 'em. Jus like them pullin' me outta them hills, all's I could do was come when they said come 'cause they trust me. It's easy to live here when they be friendly, and I shore don't want to try it if'n they was mad at a body." He turned as if he was ready to go then looked back at me and added, "Luck to ya then, Ty." With that, he walked to his mule and began cinching down the packs.

I turned to walk to my horse when he yelled, "Hey!" I turned back to face him, and he tossed me an old flintlock

Henry model 1817 pistol. "Noticed you was unheeled so I figger you ta have ma spare."

"Thanks," I replied as I shoved it behind my belt. When I walked away, I realized that I hadn't even thought about needing a gun the whole time I was here. But I didn't hesitate to load a charge in the chamber and charge the flash pan as soon as I got to my horse.

I was saddled up and ready to mount when Running Elk walked up with two women. I still didn't understand what they said, but from their tone I could imagine it was a farewell and such. I had begun to feel a kinship among these people as I never I had before. The older woman handed me a pack wrapped in a beautifully tanned elk hide, and with her hand gesturing to her mouth, I took it that the pack was full of food. I nodded my thanks.

The younger woman stepped forward and showed me a pair of knee-high moccasins unlike any I had seen before. The leather was dark tanned and smooth. The inside was fur lined with what looked like rabbit. She pointed at the rawhide thong that tied them together, and then she hung them over the saddle horn. It was then that I realized she was trying to tell that these moccasins were in trade for the lynx that I had brought with me three days earlier. She put a hand on my arm and said, "My much thank you," in a halting, broken English.

I suddenly realized that I knew this girl. I mean, I recognized her. She was the girl from the creek where I shot those three men.

My mouth fell open, and she smiled. I smiled and put a hand on her shoulder, and she repeated, "My much thank you."

I was deeply moved as never had been before. I folded my hands together and nodded toward her in a praying fashion in hopes that they could see that I accepted her thanks as well as see my gratitude to them. She responded with a huge smile, and I knew that she understood.

I left the camp with a farewell wave and higher hopes for the future.

15

The snow was melting fast, and the nights were pleasant, although I knew that there would still be some cold spells to come and possibly more snow. I took in the country around me as I rode to the east. It's hard sometimes to make yourself look around at the beauty that God has laid before us. We get wrapped up in the day-to-day struggles and don't often stop actually see what is around us. So this day, I vowed to respect and enjoy creation. And I did.

I guided the roan to the top of a rise and took a slow, long look at the hills and valleys around me. I noticed two deer feeding quietly next to a stream over a half mile away. An eagle drifted lazily overhead looking for an unsuspecting meal moving in the sparse grass below. I could also see a herd of antelope bounding over the hill to safety from an unseen predator.

Then I noticed the predator. The antelope must have just caught the scent of the wolf as she sat on the far slope as if waiting for something. I nudged the roan, and he started walking forward toward a fold in the hills close to where she sat. As I drew nearer, she stood and trotted forward as if she had been waiting for me to show up. When she was about thirty yards from us, she stopped and sat down in the grass as I pulled the roan to a stop, and we talked.

"I ain't sure that I understand all that's happened in these last days, but I kind of like it," I said. "You and me have cut quite a swath among these folks around here."

The wolf just cocked her head to the side and looked at me like she knew all along and was just waiting for me to understand.

I nudged the roan forward, and the wolf took off up the hill and kept pace with us as we traveled east toward our cabin.

The last few days with the Indians had started me to thinking about what I was doing here. Not just here and now but what had brought me here, and what was I looking for?

I had been chased across this great land by a cutthroat bunch of thieves and murderers. I had started running because of the situation, but now I realize that I have run myself right to where I belong.

What did I really want? A home, that was for certain, but I didn't just want a place to live; I needed a place to belong. And to my astonishment, I had felt that these last few days.

Whether misguided by their thoughts or truly insightful, the Indians had accepted me for who and what I was. I wasn't sure even I knew that right now.

The wolf traveled with us all through the day, sometimes within a few yards of us and sometimes beyond the ridge to left or right. The roan had begun to accept her presence, and I found myself looking for her from time to time and hoping she was close by.

That first night away from the Indians, I made a dry camp in a shallow draw that almost came to a dead end at a sheer rock face. I knew I wouldn't have to worry about security from that direction at least. I staked the roan on a picket rope about twenty feet long and put together a small hat full of fire behind a large, blown-down snag that blocked the view from the entrance of the draw. As I spread out my groundsheet next to the fire, I surely hoped that the pack contained food for I had forgotten to check. If it didn't, I would be almighty disappointed and hungry this night. I pulled the pistol from my belt, laid it close to hand, and then opened the pack. I'll admit I didn't know what to expect, but I'm positive that only the all-knowing God of heaven could have even guessed what I would find in this bundle.

There were several small hide pouches folded together containing roasted seeds, dried berries, dried roots, and close to two pounds of dried meat strips. There was also a hollow gourd filled with a mixture of dried shredded meat, dried berries, nuts, and covered with a honey glaze. Maybe this was a sort of pemmican that I had heard about. Next, I found a hide rolled into a long cylinder shape, about a foot long, and when I unrolled it, I found two dozen perfectly formed arrow heads beautifully knapped from flint. Folded smoothly under it all was the most lavish gift I could have ever expected to receive from anyone. It was a fringed elk-hide shirt expertly tanned and hand stitched with a pattern of beadwork so intricate that I could only stare in amazement. The leather was a deep golden brown that would blend in with the surrounding country.

I stripped off my sweat-stained canvas shirt and pulled the smooth, freshly tanned hide shirt over my head to see if it would fit. I should have never had a doubt that it would mold itself to my muscular frame just as if it had been sewn by a New York tailor, for the shirt had been made with caring hands that seemed to have knowing ways about them.

The shirt smelled like leather with a strong scent of wood smoke picked up in the curing and tanning process, but there were other smells there too. Smells that reminded me of different things around an Indian encampment. The shirt fit well, and it was surprisingly comfortable too. I took it off and refolded it on the groundsheet next to me and pulled my canvas shirt back on.

I chewed some of the dried meat and ate a handful of the pemmican mixture while I let my eyes wander over patterns of the stitching and the beads that adorned the shirt. Later, when I rolled up in my blankets, I had the warm feeling inside of family again. Well, a family that I was just getting to know.

The next morning found us packed and moving with the first gray streaks in the eastern sky. The roan was rested and stepping smartly in the cold, crisp morning air. I let him move at his own pace, but we stopped often to look at streams or to investigate a bluff or mesa. For the first time, I was able to appreciate the beauty and savagery of the country around me.

Because we were traveling slow and it had snowed again, it took us eight days to reach the cabin. It was still early in the day when we cautiously entered the clearing. Most of the new snow was already melted in the open area around the cabin and the barn, but the drifts against the walls would be around for a while because they tend to refreeze into hard-packed ice at night.

I studied the ground leading into the clearing and then around the barn and cabin for a few minutes before I felt somewhat comfortable that no one had been here in my absence. I also watched the ears of my horse for signs of alertness because he would know well before I would if someone was around.

I turned to look over my shoulder and spotted the wolf sitting contentedly in the shadows of the trees, simply watching. She was not on the alert either, so I felt unusually safe at the time.

I dismounted at the barn and led the roan into the stall and unloaded what was left of the pack of food received from the Indians and stripped off the saddle and bridle and hung them on the rail. I walked to the back of the stall and opened the door that led to the small corral. It occurred to me that I had never had the need to open this door before because the weather had been so cold when I first arrived. As I inspected the door and its frame, I was once again impressed with the craftsmanship that had gone into the construction this barn.

I forked some hay into the stall to keep the roan occupied for a while then started the usual rubdown with a piece of canvas.

My thoughts drifted here and there over the last months before I met the Indians, and I didn't like what I found. It seemed that fate and circumstance had ruled my actions to this point and, in turn, left me on the run. I don't regret ending up here, but I would never have a true sense of peace until I stood up for myself and quit running.

I had almost decided that this would be a good place to stay on and start over with a new life when I remembered that the previous owner may come back and claim his cabin. Although it was not uncommon to find abandoned cabins and even full farms where the owner had met some untimely fate or simply became overwhelmed by their situation, never to return.

I could not claim this kind of craftsmanship for my own. I would find a location close by and build my own home. At least, that way, I could watch over this cabin until the owner returned, and of course, I would remain close to the Indians.

I pondered that thought. I still couldn't communicate with them, but neither could Buffalo Tongue when he first met them, and now he speaks their language. They seem to respect his knowledge and his word, so hopefully they would have enough patience to teach me as well.

I walked toward the cabin, and the wolf trotted along the tree line keeping pace with me. I stepped up onto the porch and reached for the latch string when I noticed she had stopped in her tracks. Her nose rose slightly sniffing the breeze to get another whiff of the scent that had been there before.

In a single jump she turned and disappeared into the trees. Startled, I placed the hide-bound packages on the porch and drew my pistol and scanned the area for movement. Nothing.

Maybe I was being overly cautious. She had probably smelled a rabbit or some such and bounded off to investigate.

I didn't really believe that, but I could remain hopeful.

I reached behind me and opened the door. I backed into the interior shadows and crouched down. My view was restricted by the doorway, but I was not nearly as exposed as I was on the porch. I continued to watch, but after a slow minute went by, I could still see no movement. I reached through the door and brought my packages inside and placed them on the table.

I laid the makings for a fire in the stove, but didn't light it yet. I wanted to look around some more to be sure there wasn't anyone watching the cabin and waiting for me to fall into my daily routine so's they could ambush me. Placing a few strips of dried meat in my coat pocket and hanging my canteen over my shoulder, I stepped out onto the porch and closed the door. I quickly stepped off the porch on the side nearest to the barn and went around behind the cabin. After a brief pause, I darted across the clearing and into the trees.

Both trails coming to the cabin lead to the front door, so I hoped that, if I had visitors, behind the cabin would be the least likely place for anyone to be.

Well, the one from the draw that I used when I first arrived was really the only trail. The other one was the path I had used to go to the stream.

I stood still against a large tree trunk and let the sounds of the afternoon filter through my ears and scanned the area. I had heard nothing unusual and was about to move when I heard a horse nicker in the distance then the roan responded with a loud neigh.

I quickly moved to a slightly better vantage point where I could see the trails clearly. Whoever came here on that horse may still be riding him, and he might have left him tied to a tree and advanced on foot.

I had waited only a few minutes when I spotted movement on the trail from the draw. There were three horses in all, and atop each was a buckskin-clad Indian. They stopped as they entered the clearing and spoke back and forth in low tones while watching the cabin.

I lowered the pistol to my side but still kept it pointed close enough if the situation asked for it. I then stepped around the bole of the tree so that I was in plain view of all three men. The second one in line saw me first and pointed toward me as he spoke. They all turned in my direction, and the first one raised his hand in greeting. I don't recall the words he spoke, but as he started speaking, I stepped forward in their direction.

When he finished and fell silent, the last man in line started his horse toward the cabin. He rode close to the porch and hung a haunch of venison on the post with a strip of rawhide. He backed up and turned his horse to face me. He cupped his hands at his chest then extended them toward me in a sweeping gesture that indicated this to be a gift.

I clasped my hands together—right over left—in front of my chest and slightly bowed my head in thanks to let them know I was grateful. I wasn't sure what the next move should be. Do I invite them for a meal? Was I supposed to cook the meat for them?

After a slow minute passed and I made no move, they turned and rode back the way they had come. I realized that I needed very much to be able to communicate with these Indians if I intended to make this my home. Then slow dawning came to me that I had not seen those three Indians before this day. When I had awoke in the lodge that last time, there had been but four men present, including Running Elk. These may have come from the main village where the celebration had taken place, but I simply could not recall seeing them before.

When they were gone and the forest sounds had returned to normal, I went back to the cabin. I lit the fire I had laid in the stove earlier and seated myself at the table with the door open, simply watching the trail, contemplating. As I have mentioned before, I'm not much of the planning sort, so my contemplating usually means sorting out what just happened so I could get my head wrapped around where I stand.

I surely was wishing that I had some coffee to help me concentrate, but it had been nearly a month since my last cup.

After a time, when the ideas of understanding began to take root in my thinking, I was interrupted by my stomach grumbling. Taking out my skillet, I went to the porch and cut a fair-sized slab from the venison haunch. I started to turn to go inside when I remembered the wolf. She wasn't in sight, but I cut a chunk for her and dropped it on the edge of the porch.

Closing the door behind me, I placed the skillet on the stove, and then I sliced up some of the dried roots and added it to the skillet along with some pemmican, and soon the cabin began to smell like a high-class restaurant. At least, what I remembered of one after so long on the trail.

The cabin warmed as I satisfied my intestinal arguments with large bites of fresh meat and washed it down with cold water from my canteen. These last slow days had almost completely healed my injuries. There were still a few sore spots and a couple of fading bruises, but I would imagine that such a fall may take weeks to heal up and hair over.

After I had emptied the skillet, I cleaned it and set it back on the shelf. I then went about the daily cleaning and straightening that is required in such a small space even if one did live alone.

I needed to check my snare line and reset the ones that showed signs of activity. Since I hadn't been there in what was going on six days, I was worried. I don't hold to senseless killing, and to trap an animal then leave him there would go hard with me. This had been on my mind since I had been escorted away by Running Elk.

When I went outside onto the porch, I almost automatically looked for the wolf in the trees. The meat I had left was still there, so I was immediately concerned.

Maybe she had caught a rabbit or some such and just wasn't hungry.

I adjusted my coat and hat and went to the barn to check on the roan. He seemed to be okay, but he was standing inside dozing in a three-legged stance with his head hanging. He jerked his head up when I entered the barn but just looked at me.

I decided then since the weather was hanging at or above freezing that I would let him rest and just walk to the stream and fill the bucket and canteen. I was not in need of meat, but if I had an easy, clean kill with the old flint lock pistol, I could always come back and get the roan to pack the meat. When I said as much, he showed his disinterest by lowering his head and closing his eyes again.

Ornery old cuss anyway. I try to treat him like a partner, and he gets all high and mighty sometimes. So I rolled my eyes in contempt at him and folded my arms in frustration. I might have even stomped my foot. I looked back out of the corner of my eye to see if he was about to apologize, but he never even opened his eyes.

You can't argue with someone who won't argue back, so I took the bucket in my left hand and my canteen hanging by a strap over my shoulder and left the barn. Walking would give me a better chance to look for the wolf anyway. At least, that's what I told myself. I'm not sure the roan would let me ride anyway. He gets kind of opinionated sometimes.

I was had almost made it to the stream when I realized that I had been so caught up in my thoughts about the roan and the wolf that I hadn't even been looking around me for signs of danger. I stopped quickly next to a large tree and listened. There was a slight wind blowing in the tree tops and a few birds chirping nearby. On occasion I could hear the call of a far-off crow. I slowly began to relax as I scanned the shadows deep within the trees.

I took my time as I covered the last fifty yards to the stream, and I approached the hole in the ice with caution. This would be a spot where someone would be apt to expect my return, so I had to be wary.

I walked out onto the ice slowly, and I could hear the sounds of the thinning ice begin to crack under my feet. It wouldn't be long before this ice would be gone because of the warming temperatures and the running water underneath. When I heard the first cracks, I retreated to the trees and found a stout limb about seven feet long. At least, if I happened to fall through the ice, the limb would be spanning across the hole and give me something to hang on to. I squatted next to the hole, and with my knife, I began to chip away at the thin ice layer on the water.

If I fell through and the water under the ice was moving fast, I would immediately be pulled away from the hole by the current. As long as I could keep my grip on this limb, if I fell into the cold, near-freezing water, I might have a chance at survival.

After a few minutes, I lowered the bucket into the hole and filled it. Then setting it aside, I removed my canteen and poured it out, removing any stale, brackish-tasting water, and refilled it with the fresh water from the stream.

With that done, I hung the canteen around my shoulder and dragged the bucket away from the hole and stood up. As I walked toward the bank, I noticed the wolf standing in the trees near the trail. I spoke to her, but she seemed nervous or scared. She kept looking back down the trail toward the cabin.

I walked in her direction until I was twenty feet from her, and then setting the bucket down, I squatted on my heels and offered her a strip of jerky that the Indians had made.

She let out a couple of excited yips and bounced on her front feet then turned and disappeared into the trees.

I spoke out loud to anyone listening: "What in tarnation has gotten into her?"

I stood staring in the direction she ran and worried a bite of the jerky loose with my teeth. When a slow minute of chewing and contemplating had gone by with no answers, I grabbed the bucket by the rope handle and started down the trail. I kept watch on both sides of the trail as I walked just in case it might have been a bear or mountain lion that the wolf had smelled.

I held the chunk of jerky in my right and the bucket in my left. I figured I could drop the dried meat and grab the pistol fast enough if the need came calling, so I continued on. My mind drifted as I walked back to the Indians and the way they all seemed to enjoy having me in their camp.

I would have to make a real effort to start learning their tongue and their hand signs. I was really warming to the idea of staying on here, and if I had the Indians to teach me a few things, I should get by. I could trap a few furs for trading, and maybe during the summer I could scout for a gold or silver deposit, although sometimes lead and sulphur could be just as valuable.

Yes, sir. I think the first thing I would do is build a shed-type roof attached to the side of the cabin to keep the ice and snow off of the wood stack. Then I would have to...

I heard a shout.

I was about eighty yards from the clearing at the cabin, and I could hear voices.

I dropped the bucket and drew my pistol as I ducked into the deeper shadows to my left.

Then I heard another shout. "I know you're in there. Come on out."

I eased forward keeping large trees between me and the cabin.

"We have the house surrounded, and we ain't leavin'," the voice continued.

I could see three men spread out in front of the cabin, and all held rifles in their hands. The talker had on a long, black frock coat and derby hat. I thought he might have been one of the gents from the boardwalk in New Orleans, but I wasn't sure. It had been a while ago, and that fracas happened at night.

Then he shouted, "This is Ben Lanauxe. I'm here to kill you, Matthews. You got a choice: you can come out and take your chances with a gun or we can burn you out."

He turned his head and spoke to the scrawny, redheaded man on his right, "Where's Jake?"

The redhead spat in the mud and snow then said, "Coverin' tha back like you said, Mr. Lanauxe."

The one called Jake must have heard his name because he came around the corner and said, "I'm here, Ben. They ain't no door nor even a window in the back, so he's gotta come out this-a-way."

"All right," Ben replied, "grab some brush and stack it in front of the door. We'll burn him where he sits, hiding in there like the coward he is."

I was still in shock that they were here and even more shocked at my good fortune of being caught outside. I would turn and run.

No. I had nowhere to run to. Without the roan, I wouldn't make it five, maybe six miles. And then what? I would still be on foot and alone. If they burned the cabin, they probably wouldn't stop there. They'd burn the barn too.

I looked at my pistol. That would be no good. Yes, I had my shooting pouch, but all I had was a single-shot flintlock pistol. It would take at least half a minute to reload. They would be on me before I could fire a second shot.

Maybe if I killed Ben with that first shot, maybe the rest would leave with their leader dead.

I knew they wouldn't. They would push all the harder to kill me. And what if I missed that first shot? If I didn't kill Ben?

I was stuck. They would fire the cabin then take the roan. They might kill him.

No, I couldn't let that happen. I had to do something. If they led the Roan out, I'd shoot the man holding him. Then he could run. But would he?

If he was scared, maybe.

"Think," I told myself.

So I yelled—well, kind of yelled—I leaned my head back and howled.

It sounded convincing to me. I was hoping these were all city boys with no experience of the timber wolf.

They were all silent and looking around into the trees with nervous glances trying to locate the source. Only about five seconds passed when, bless my soul, that she wolf howled from the trees not a hundred yards behind them.

Nobody seemed too overly concerned until there was the scream of frightened horses in the shadows of the trail.

Ben turned toward the sound and hissed, "Simms, you keep that door covered with that rifle. Jake, you and Deke go get them horses. We can't lose them."

Jake and Deke scrambled for the trail and had just barely missed being run over by six horses running wide-eyed at full gallop. There were four saddled horses, and two barebacked horses that looked like they had been carrying packs, and each one had long blood smears streaming down their sides. They ran through the clearing then down the trail past me toward the stream.

Deke had been knocked to the ground next to a large spruce with its boughs hanging low and sweeping the ground. He rolled onto his stomach and was starting to rise when he was grabbed by the foot.

He screamed as he was jerked under the trees where he completely disappeared. He let out another loud choking scream then suddenly went silent.

Jake spun and fired into the tree but there was no further sound.

The three remaining men huddled together quickly then turned toward me, scrambling in the direction of the running horses. They had moved no more than ten steps when Simms, who was the last man in the line, suddenly screamed, throwing up his hands, falling facedown in the mud and snow. When I looked closer, I could see an arrow shaft protruding from his back.

This whole scene had unfolded in less than five minutes, and I had been kneeling behind this tree all the while. I quickly stood and moved around the tree so that I could cover the trail with my pistol.

Either Ben or Jake must have seen movement because a bullet came through the tree just a few inches above my head. Small bits of wood and bark peppered the side of my face, and I instinctively dove to the ground.

When I crawled back to my knees and peered through the trees, I could see both men running straight toward me with guns extended. Since they had seen me move, they shifted their focus from the horses assuming that I was the reason that men were dying. I shifted on my knees to the other side of the tree.

Both men were about ten feet apart when they slid to a stop thirty feet from me. Jake stepped to the left so that Ben wouldn't be in his line of fire and raised his gun.

I was still on my knees behind the tree, and when I leaned to the side to get a look around the branches, I was suddenly face to face with Ben Lanauxe. I could see in the man's eyes that he wanted me dead in the worst way.

"Well, well, well," Ben said with a malicious smile, "Mr. Matthews. So you weren't inside the house after all." He glanced back at Jake then stepped to his right to get himself further out of the line of fire.

"I'm gonna kill him, Ben," Jake said "So you best get your talkin' done."

Ben chuckled and said, "We have chased you a long way for what you have done to my family. You shot my pa. Then you killed my brother Jim and his boy with that rock slide, and I'm not a forgiving man. The end result today is you being dead, and I don't much care how it happens or who does it. If Jake here doesn't kill you first, then I'll see you hang before the days over. I'm going to see to it personally and make sure it gets finished."

I closed my hand expecting to feel the grip of my pistol, but it closed into a tight fist. I must have dropped it when I dove. I knew I had to move and I hoped that I could dive out of the line of fire and then run. But before I could move, Jake raised his rifle and tightened his finger on the trigger. Then just as suddenly, he stiffened and let the rifle fall to the ground.

He looked down at the arrowhead that appeared in the center of his chest. The arrow shaft drove through him from behind when he fell onto his back in the trail.

Ben looked back at the sound of Jake's body hitting the ground. He let out a furious growl of frustration as he turned back to face me and started to raise his own rifle. Just then, his attention was shifted by a sudden flurry of movement.

There was another rush of horses coming back from the stream, and as they ran by, an Indian hanging low down on the side of one of the horses reached out and buried a tomahawk into Ben's neck. He fell to the ground gasping for breath. He looked around quickly with fear in his eyes. "How many…" he muttered. He gulped a ragged breath as he looked back at me and asked, "Who the devil are you?"

He died just like that.

Now, I'm not sure if he was asking who I was because he was knocked senseless and he didn't remember, or if he just couldn't figure why anyone would help a two-by-twice nobody like me. He probably had convinced himself through his own self-importance that he could kill me with no more thought than slapping a mosquito.

It didn't matter to me; I was still standing, and he was dead, along with every man jack that he brought with him.

Two Indian warriors came cautiously out of the trees with bows at the ready. I lifted my right hand and said, "No need to worry, friend. He's dead."

I bent down and scooped up my pistol. When I opened the frizzen, I found that it was packed full of snow from the fall. I never would have gotten off a shot anyway. I breathed a heavy sigh of relief. Was it really over? Would I forever be looking over my shoulder or did it end with Ben? It would be a long time before I found out the truth of that.

When I walked back into the clearing around the cabin, I should have been shocked, but after the last week, I just smiled. There were five or six Indians coming out of the trees that I could see. Two were coming through the trees around the barn; three were clustered together pointing toward the horses talking in low tones. Powder Keg approached me apparently to see if I was injured. He smiled and grasped my forearm with a handshake I had seen among the Indians before.

I was finding it to be more and more bothersome that I couldn't communicate with the Indians. I tried several ways to show my gratitude and thanks, but I never could be sure they understood. Buffalo Tongue assured me that body language and hand signs would be enough for now, but I had to wonder.

The remainder of the day was spent moving the bodies, and, yes, I gave them a Christian burial even though they probably didn't deserve it. Truthfully, though, that part is up to God to sort out. I'd just do my part and leave the rest up to Him.

As I was going about this gruesome task, I caught the stares of several Indians. Did they not bury their enemies? Did they simply drag them away and leave them to the scavengers? They had no thoughts about taking the boots and hats, a coat from one man, and the rifles and gun belts.

Maybe they were just as curious about my actions and rituals as I was of theirs, how I buried them or why I lifted my eyes toward the heavens and spoke over these criminals.

The Indians stayed close by for several days after the attack. They spent their time hunting close by and had brought me another haunch of venison even before the first one was completely gone. I found that I had no items or skills to give in return, so I concentrated on bonding more with the wolf. This seemed to continually fascinate the warriors. They would sit and watch as I fed her scraps or bits of meat and marvel at my conversations with her even though they had no idea what I was saying.

At first, I felt that my actions simply provided a novelty for them, but these were sharp, intelligent men. They seemed to understand the connection even more than I did, so I tried to make it a point to be as earnest and upfront as I could with my action. They would lose all trust if they thought I was dishonest or misleading them in any way.

On the morning of the fourth day, after I had buried the dead, the Indians packed up their meat supplies and waved their departing so longs as they headed back to their own lodges.

I'll admit, I was sad to see them go. I had learned a few words of their language and enjoyed the company in spite of the lack of communication.

After lunch, I picked up my bow given to me by one of the Indians and a quiver of arrows. Today, I would explore, hunt, and, hopefully, find my lost guns. I went to the barn and opened the door. The roan was looking at me like he thought I had forgotten he existed.

"I've been sort of busy," I said. He never asked questions of the future, but I thought he should know, so I said, "It's just you and me now." I scratched his neck under his mane and said, "I hope you've had enough rest, old pard'. You and me are going to start fixing up our new home, and if the previous owner comes back, he can bunk out here with you." I smiled. "Then I need to find that Walker Colt that you made me drop in that snow slide."

He just shook his head and blew like he was trying to say, "Here we go again."

Some folk just ain't never happy.

CPSIA information can be obtained
at www.ICGtesting.com
Printed in the USA
FFOW05n0901141016